W.

Milton Hicks was a real warrior of old Texas, a breed Cherokee who had fought with Andy Jackson in Louisiana against the Red Sticks. He came to Texas and continued to follow the path of the gun. Not much is known about him, other than that he was a brave man and a resourceful fighter. He never owned land, voted, married, or joined the Catholic Church (which was necessary for citizenship in this state of old Mexico). He died in battle with the Comanche.

Now this hero of the Old West is brought to searing life by his descendant, Captain D. L. "Pappy" Hicks, a modern-day hero who fought in Korea, led the Montagnards of the Central Highlands in Vietnam against the Viet Cong, and was famed as a master of the Gurkha kukri knife, "The Great Silencer."

Only a historian, guerrilla fighter, and master storyteller could have brought Milton Hicks to epic life.

KWAHARIE

Captain D. L. "Pappy" Hicks

A DELL BOOK

Published by
Dell Publishing
a division of
The Bantam Doubleday Dell Publishing Group, Inc.
1 Dag Hammarskjold Plaza
New York, New York 10017

Dell® TM 681510, Dell Publishing, a division of the
Bantam Doubleday Dell Publishing Group, Inc.

ISBN: 0-440-20019-9

Printed in the United States of America

May 1988

10 9 8 7 6 5 4 3 2 1

OPM

MILTON HICKS:
A Character Sketch.

Milton Hicks is a dim figure in Texas history, but some factual information about him does exist.

He was the grandson of Chief Charles Hicks, Principal Chief of the Cherokee nation until his death in 1827. Milton was born about 1798 in the Cherokee nation, which is now Tennessee.

When the Cherokees joined Jackson's army to fight against the Red Sticks of the Creek nation in the War of 1812, Milton went along as a young warrior of about sixteen years of age. After the Red Sticks were vanquished, most of the Cherokees went home. A few others, Milton included, went with Jackson to New Orleans. After the war, Milton came to Texas.

There is little documentation on what Milton Hicks did in Texas. There is no evidence that he ever married, owned land, voted, owed debts, held public office, served on a jury, was ever arrested, or converted to Catholicism, which was required by both Spanish and Mexican law for a person to become a citizen of Mexico.

The only documents in which Milton Hicks figures are as a man of the gun as a member of some armed force. He fought against Indians with the Spanish, Mexican, and Texas Republic governments. It can be assumed that to be a gunslinger was his only vocation.

He was a member of the Anglo settlers' army that captured Fort Velasco, June 1832. His leg was shattered in that battle.

In January 1839, he was killed along with thirteen other men in a group called the "Webster party." The group was ambushed by Comanche Indians on Brushy Creek, just north of present-day Austin, Texas. When the party was found, all that remained was their skeletons. It was determined that it was the Webster party that had been found because of Milton Hicks' broken leg.

No one knows Texas, or war, better than Captain D. L. "Pappy" Hicks. He has walked and ridden over every mile of the country his ancestor, Milton Hicks, fought over. He has also spilled his own blood, and that of others, in conventional wars, guerrilla wars, and intelligence operations on three continents.

Chapter One

The tall buckskin-clad man rode into Nacogdoches from the north on an unshod Plains Indian pony. A floppy, large-brimmed felt hat that had seen many days' trail use protected his dark face from the hot midday sun. He rode past the old stone house, which was already famous in this small settlement in the eastern part of the Mexican state of Tejas, called Texas by the Anglo settlers.

It appeared that the tall man never looked to the right or left, but his keen eyes took in everything in one quick sweep, his mind cataloging and filing away everything he saw. He took note of the sleepy hound lying in shade under the porch. The dog raised its eyelids just enough to watch horse and rider pass. If it had not been so hot, it would have run out, barked, and nipped at the heels of these newcomers. One man lay asleep at the end of a porch, and another nodded his head from a nearby chair. Some of the Anglo settlers were quick to adopt the Mexican custom of an afternoon siesta. Neither of the men raised his head as the horse and rider passed. A cloud of fine dust hung over the empty street like a low-hanging fog as the pair passed.

When the big man brought his mount to a halt in front of a large building, which housed a general mercantile store and a saloon, the animal gave a visible, shuddering sigh of relief as Milton stepped down from the Mexican saddle. The brawny little pony was of the Spanish "barb" line of Moorish Arabian horse, and could carry a rider all day and night at a canter if necessary. But it was used to carrying the small, wiry Plains Indians and not this giant of a man. It would be a pleasure to stand hipshot at a hitching post for a while, even if it would be in the hot, broiling sun.

Everything Milton Hicks owned was tied to the saddle on his horse. An Indian trade blanket, a linen shirt, and a beautiful Cherokee-made buckskin jacket with a panther, called a *tlvdatsi* by the Cherokee, painted on its back. The panther was his animal of destiny.

All of these were rolled in a piece of buckskin to protect them from the weather. In his saddlebags he carried a small bag of salt, some jerked venison and bear meat wrapped in doeskin, and extra gunpowder and lead shot for his rifle and pistol. A small leather pouch at the bottom of one bag contained 89 American dollars and 196 Mexican pesos. Not much for some, but enough for a footloose frontiersman.

From the saddle horn hung a pouch made of soft doeskin containing the only thing that linked Milton Hicks with the white man's civilization. It was one of twelve silver goblets with the family crest engraved on its side that his white grandfather had brought to the American colonies from England. It was a symbol that his white ancestors were also great warriors. One of the Hicks' ancestors had earned the crest when knighted by Richard of the Lion Heart during the Crusades.

He carried a long-barreled Pennsylvania-made rifle with percussion lock cradled in the crook of his left arm. The rifle was too long for use while mounted on a horse, but he had been a woodsman and traveled most of his life on foot, as did most Indians of the mountains, before coming to Texas. Also, he favored the rifle over the short musket, the rifle allowing him to shoot at a greater distance and with more accuracy. Powder horn and pouch with shot and percussion caps hung across his chest. A pistol was tucked in his belt and a large-bladed bowie knife hung at his right side. Jim Bowie had given Milton the knife when the young knife fighter had come to Texas two years earlier. A much-used, dented, and scarred tomahawk was also stuck in his belt.

Milton took long strides up the steps and onto the porch of the store, his Cherokee moccasins making no noise. Three Anglo-Americans sitting on the porch nodded a greeting as he walked past. The tall man gave a curt nod in return.

"Don't see many Plains Injun ponies carrin' a Meskin saddle up in this here part of Texas," one of the three said.

The others nodded agreement.

Milton walked into the open door and over to the bar that ran alongside a wall. He carried his rifle, and when he walked up to the bar he did not lean it against a wall but kept it cradled in the crook of his left arm.

The proprietor of the store was an American who had come to Texas a few years earlier. He walked from the back of the store and around behind the bar. He greeted Milton. "How do?"

"*Cerveza.*" Milton used the Spanish word for beer.

"How things be with you, Mr. Hicks?" the store owner asked.

Milton gave a short "Good."

The owner took the lid off a large wooden barrel and dipped a glass mug into the warm, home-brewed beer. He wiped off the bottom of the mug and sat it in front of Milton.

"You been up to the Cherokee village?" the store owner asked.

"Yep."

"Seen ole Tecumseh up there?"

"Yep."

Tecumseh was the name given Tom Bell after the Battle of the Thames during the War of 1812. Some claimed that Bell was the one who had killed the great war chief of the Shawnee, Tecumseh. Bell never said anything one way or the other, and he was one of those men you didn't push for an answer. Tom Bell was another one of those white men who preferred to live in the wilds with the red men. During the winter months he spent much of his time with the tribe of Cherokee that had migrated to Texas a number of years ago. One of the women of the tribe was his wife. It didn't bother him that he had a white wife in the United States whom he had failed to divorce. A man got lonesome living alone in the woods, and he

needed someone to keep the fires burning and cook the meat
he brought to the lodge. The Cherokee themselves didn't mind
having among them a white man who had killed an Indian
war chief, even if that war chief was half Cherokee. The Shawnee were traditional enemies of the Cherokee, and Tecumseh
had chosen to be a Shawnee.

"Tecumseh? Why he wuz kilt up in Canady more'n seventeen year ago," one of the four men at the end of the bar said.

Milton had noticed the four when he first came in and
couldn't help but hear them. They were strangers to him and
couldn't have been in the country long. That spring the Mexican government had passed a law that was known as the Law
of 1830, banning any more settlers from coming into Mexico
from other countries. The law was against all immigration,
but it was aimed at the Americans who were flooding the
country. The law was hard to enforce. The borders with the
United States were long, and the Mexican army was small on
the frontiers of northeastern Mexico. Men like these four
loudmouths were beginning to filter into Texas more and
more. They were not of the high caliber of Anglos who made
up the Austin colony down Brazoria way, nor were they the
same type of men who had come to Texas even a few years
earlier.

Milton ignored the men.

"Tecumseh is a white man by the name of Tom Bell," the
store owner informed the men. He looked at Milton, then at
the four men. "He is up at the Cherokee village of Chief
Bowl."

One of the men spit a stream of tobacco juice onto the saw-
dust-covered floor. Tobacco stains ran from his lower lip and
down his unkept beard. He growled, "Them damn Cherokee!
We got enough trouble with 'em heatherns over in Georgie.
We don't need 'em over here. An' a white man thet would live
amongst 'em heatherns ain't no more'n a savage hisself."

The men laughed, and one slapped him on the back. The
Beard beamed with his importance.

"Yeah, an' them redskin heatherns is trying to act like they wuz white men back in Georgie so's we God-fearin' men can't run 'em off their land," the tall, skinny one put in. He couldn't be outdone by The Beard. "An' all them Yankee preachers from up North missionarin' among 'em to make Christian folks outta 'em savages oughta be run outta the country, too. Everybody knows 'em Injuns ain't got no more soul than a nigger."

The trashy men began to warm to the subject, each trying to outdo the other.

"Yeah, them Injuns over in Georgie is tryin' to get whitened up so's they kin stay on thet land an' keep us real God-fearin' white folks from takin' it an' puttin' it to use." The Beard spoke loud enough for all to hear. "But we white folks ain't gonna let no heathern redskins set on thet mountain o' gold they's got over there in Georgie."

Skinny slapped his hand on the bar top. "Thet's for a certain fact. An' Andy Jackson says we kin have that land as soon as them Cherokee is moved. 'Sides, them heatherns ain't got no use for thet gold. Jest a skin hut, a piece of red meat, an' a lotta booze is all they need."

This brought more howls of laughter.

The store owner looked at the four men and slowly shook his head, hoping it would shut their loud mouths. He wasn't worried about the four men, but he didn't care to see his business wrecked. He looked at Hicks, knowing he had to do something or there was going to be killing here on this day.

"Where you bound to?" he asked, minding someone else's business.

"San Antonio de Bexar," Milton told him, looking straight ahead.

"Need some supplies, Mr. Hicks?"

"Coffee, maybe," Milton said, draining the mug and setting it down in front of him. He signaled for one more beer.

"How about some salt?"

"Got some." Milton still didn't look in the direction of the four men.

The store owner knew Milton Hicks both personally and by

reputation. The tall man was ready for action at all times on a moment's notice and would kill as quickly as it took a hungry cat to lick the cream off his whiskers. There were a few men who were willing to give a life to take a life. This breed Indian was one of them.

He walked to the end of the bar where the four men stood. He looked at them a moment, then shrugged his shoulders and walked to the other side of the store.

God! If these men can't read a man like Milton Hicks, they gonna be in a heap of trouble in this here part of the world, the store owner thought. He knew there were a lot of Milton Hickses in Texas. Most of them were quiet, gentle-acting men who would go the distance to help a friend, or even a stranger. But when pushed or their honor was compromised, they became wild madmen that only death itself could stop. It seemed that these four didn't have sense enough to know real trouble until it hit them square in their faces. Yes, there were a lot of riffraff and frontier trash coming into Texas lately.

"Hey, mister, you one of 'em squaw men like yore frien', thet Tom 'Tecumseh' Bell?" The Beard called to Milton. "See yore wearin' buckskins an' moccasins made by 'em Cherokee."

"Can't say as I blame him, Fred. It gits down right lonesome out in the woods. An' some of 'em Cherokee squaws is mitey fine-lookin' wimmin', even if they is Injuns," laughed Skinny, making vulgar gestures.

"They may not have souls like our white wimmin', but some of 'em sure got the tits like 'em," Fred snickered.

"An' lak I found out long ago, be they black, red, or white, they's all got the same thing between their legs," the third man put in. He was being left out.

There were more loud laughs and pounding on the bar top. Milton drank some more of his warm beer.

"Why, he ain't even looked our way oncet. Maybe he's been squawin' so long he can't talk American no more," Skinny informed his friends with an important air.

The men laughed again. Four on one isn't bad odds.

The store owner brought a small bag of coffee over to the

bar and set it down in front of Milton. "Be anything else, Mr. Hicks?"

Milton grumbled a "No" and drank his beer.

The owner walked down the long bar and stopped in front of the four men. He had sawdust on the floor, but blood was still messy.

"That big man is Milton Hicks and he won't take too kindly to you talkin' 'bout the Cherokee that way," he told them. He knew it was a lost cause before he started, but he was the type who had to try.

"Oh, yeah? An' what you call him 'mister' for, George?" Fred asked. "Hell! He looks more heathern Injun than white."

"He's got more Cherokee blood than white. An' I gotta say this, although it ain't none of my business, but you men are 'bout to bite off more than you kin chew. He took a strong look at all four of you. He'd know you a huntert years from now if he saw you in hell," George informed them.

"Thet's jest where he mite git to see us next. An' you called thet half-breed 'mister.' We ain't in the habit of callin' 'em red heathern 'mister' down in Georgie." Fred spat out the word as if he had tasted something bitter.

"We ain't over in North Carolina either," George told the four men. "We're down here in Mexico now. An' there's a lot more Indians in Texas than there are white, be they Spanish white or American white. Besides, I call this man 'mister' 'cause he is one."

"Ha! He ain't even talkin'. He's jest a stinkin' red heathern thet don't know nothin' from nothin'," Skinny put in.

"Yeah?" George asked. "I don't know a lot about this man. Most don't. But I do know he's smart. He speaks English, Spanish, French, Cherokee, Comanche, and who knows what else. How many do you boys speak?"

"He may be a rough, tough breed, but the're four of us," Fred said with all the bluster he could muster.

"Sir, I don't want to keep buttin' into your business, but he will quietly kill all four of you, pay for the damages, an' just as quietly get on thet little pony of his an' ride off." George walked back down the bar, muttering to himself, "Some men never learn."

"Hey! You! Injun boy!" Fred called. "I ain't never seed no Injun walk right up to a bar an' drink like no white man 'afore. They always gave them redskins their rotgut in the woods back home. Reckon the law is a mite different down here in Mexico. These here Meskins thinks 'em redskins is real folks."

An' they don't sell Indians booze 'cause all it does is cause trouble, the store owner thought. Well, what have we got here? A killin' in the makin' by drunk whites.

Milton finished his beer and placed the mug back on the bar. He nodded to George and walked into the middle of the floor and turned to face the four men. Milton stood relaxed, the rifle still in the crook of his left arm. He looked hard at all four of the men. The killing was about to begin.

"Gentlemen, you will say that the Cherokee are the most honorable people you have ever seen, or I will kill all four of you where you stand." The statement was made in a slow, quiet voice.

A challenge had been made and an ultimatum given that required only an affirmative response to stay the promised act of violence. The affair had suddenly taken a turn that would either require these loudmouthed braggarts to prove their mettle or back down.

The small, sickly-looking one now wished that he had remained in camp by the river that day as he had wanted to. He had felt ill even before leaving camp that morning. Now he felt even worse, and the whiskey he had drunk did nothing to stiffen his backbone.

The other three suddenly became aware that this man would not back down and they would have to fight for their lives. They were now in Mexico, where even an Indian had the right to protect himself. And worse, they were in Mexico illegally. These men were of the frontier themselves, and tough in the ways of a rough world. But the quiet strength of this big man became ominous in this hot room that had suddenly become smaller. But they had nothing to worry about. Like a pack of dogs, they knew there was safety in numbers. This man was nothing but a breed anyway, so why worry?

The first words Fred spoke came tight in his throat, but he tried to force them out to sound tough and commanding. "Mister, the're four of us here. You ain't got no more chance than a pat of butter on a hot stove. I think you aughta ride on outta here whilst you kin."

"All four of you are carrying pistols and knives. I suggest you look to yourselves, gentlemen," Milton told them. He looked at Fred. "An' you, sir, will be the first to die."

Without a pause the sickly-looking man screamed "God!" and pulled his pistol. His one and only shot was wide of its mark.

Meanwhile the lead ball from Milton's rifle hit Fred in the forehead between the eyes. The ball tore a large hole out of the top part of the back of his head as it passed through. Splinters of bone from the skull and brains splattered on the sickly-looking man, who had ducked behind Fred for protection. The sickly man emptied the whiskey he had drunk that day upon the floor.

Milton shifted the rifle to his left hand and drew his big knife by its handle. He threw it and it stuck in the throat of Skinny, the second-loudest of the four. The blade slashed through his voice box, turning his scream into a squeaking gurgle of death. The tall man shot the fourth man in the chest with his pistol.

The sickly-looking man tried to run past Milton in his effort to escape. The heavy barrel caught the man at the base of the skull and cracked it like a housewife cracking an eggshell. The little man gave his last scream and fell to the floor in a crumpled heap.

In less than ten seconds three men were dead and another lay bleeding to death with a bullet hole in his chest. The man gurgled with each breath and a small bubble of blood appeared in his left nostril and burst.

Three men dead and one dying, and Milton had not drawn

his favorite weapon, the *galuyasti usdi*, "little ax" or "toma-hawk."

Milton put his pistol back in his belt and walked over to the man with the knife in his throat. After pulling it loose, he wiped the blade on the man's dirty shirt and placed it in its sheath. He then walked over to the bar and threw a gold piece on its top. "See that those that are dead get buried. Take some for cleanin' up the floor. Tell the alcalde I'm on my way to de Bexar if he wants me."

"I'm sure he won't. It was a fair fight. Four against one," George said.

Without another word, Milton pushed his way past the three men standing and gawking, wide-eyed, at the door, got on his horse and rode out of town.

No, the alcalde of Nacogdoches would not want to see Milton Hicks about the killings. George would say it was self-defense, and his word was good enough for anyone. It was a fight of four against one. Four fools who decided to take on Milton Hicks. The Mexicans were people of honor and under-stood self-defense. And no Mexican liked illegal Americans.

Chapter Two

Milton guided his horse through the main part of town, around the Plaza Principal, past Thorn's Mercantile, Sim's Saloon, the Red House, which was headquarter's for Colonel Piedras of the Mexican army, and straight out of the small frontier town.

The small settlement of three hundred or so souls was the most important outpost on the East Texas frontier. It was militarily important as well as being the center for trade. Its architectural structure was typical of villages in the forest region of Texas. The Mexicans did not build their log houses in the manner of the Americans but in the manner of most American Indians. The design of the frontier Mexicans were called picket huts. The houses were constructed by placing logs in the ground to stand upright and then filling the open spaces between the logs with mud. Palmetto leaves or rawhide served to cover the roofs. These were the homes of the peons. Mexicans of means lived in houses of milled lumber, thick stone walls, or brick. No matter where in Mexico the town was located, there were always the flat-roofed adobe buildings the Spanish had adopted from the Pueblo Indian.

Milton rode down the dirt street, looking neither left nor right. Men who knew him spoke as he passed. The big man nodded acknowledgment. It did not bother these men, most of whom were Mexicans, that Milton didn't stop and greet them as long-lost friends. They knew it was not his nature to yell and wave.

A dog ran out into the street, ready to bark and nip at the horse's heels. Instead it sniffed the wild, untamed scent of the little pony and its equally untamed rider, turned, and slunk back under a chair in front of a log hut where it could bark and growl from safety. If there had been other dogs it would have let the world know of its presence. The dog was like most men Milton knew. He was brave only when his anonymity was assured by a crowd.

Milton left the town behind and guided his horse out onto the famous Camino Real, an old road that had once been an Indian trading trail. The Spanish had used the road to link Mexico City to her frontier colonies. The Camino Real, the "Royal Road," ran from coast to coast in two segments. One road ran northwest from Mexico City and ended in San Francisco. The other ran to the northeast out of Mexico City and ended in the old Spanish town of Saint Augustine on the Atlantic coast. This road linked the Texas towns of San Antonio, Alto, and Nacogdoches with Mexico City. From Nacogdoches Milton would be in the saddle for over 300 miles before reaching San Antonio de Bexar.

He kicked the small horse into a fast, smooth, ground-eating dogtrot that the animal could keep all day. By nightfall Milton would camp on the banks of the Neches River some thirty-five miles to the west. He was not really in a hurry to reach his destination. A frontiersman did not hurry unless there was a reason. Milton had no real purpose for going to San Antonio except for a few friends and a woman he would see—and a change of scenery, the food of life for footloose men of the time.

Milton was a tall man, standing six feet four inches. About three-fourths Cherokee, he had inherited his height from his Indian ancestors. The Europeans were surprised when they had first encountered the Cherokee. These observers reported that the people of this Indian tribe were much taller than the average European, who was about five feet six inches at the time. Milton's great-grandfather was Nathan Hicks, a government trader for the British in the mid 1700s. From him he got his English ancestry and his weight. His hawklike nose and swarthy complexion were Cherokee. His hair was black and straight, cut just above his collar. What surprised strangers when they saw him in Indian dress was his eyes. They were white man's eyes, light blue, except when angered. When angered, the eyes turned steel-gray, the only outward appearance of emotion he ever showed the world. It took a brave man to stand firm under the stare of those cold, hard eyes. Or a fool.

The tall man was easygoing and quiet by outward disposition, letting others live as they pleased. But just beneath the surface of this thin veneer of civil restraint was a wild, cunning, individualistic man of nature.

He had been born in the mountains of Tennessee along the banks of the Little Tennessee River. This was the home of the Overhill Cherokee. Shortly after his birth, he was taken south by his mother to the Tennessee–Georgia border area. The land of the Cherokee was being taken by more and more whites moving into their territory. The Cherokee nation had once claimed an extensive part of the western and southern present-day United States, around the Great Smoky Mountains. The whites were still pushing, and Milton knew that his red family would have no land east of the Mississippi River before long. The white man's lust for land was beyond belief.

Milton had been educated in the white man's way. His grandfather, the chief, had insisted on this for all his grandchildren. It wasn't that the old man thought very highly of his father's white society, but he knew it was in the best interests of his children and the Cherokee nation that future generations know the language and ways of the white man.

In these schools run by Moravian missionaries, Milton had learned to read and write English, French, and Spanish; he also had a working knowledge of Latin and ancient Greek. The churchmen wanted to prove that these children of the forest could learn as well as any white child. Many white people thought it was a waste of time to teach savages such refinements.

The young boy grew up under dual teachings. At home his Cherokee teacher taught him the ways of the Cherokee and how the world was made by Asgaya Galulati for the animals of the Sky Rock. Man did not come down from the Sky Rock until after the animals and plants.

Milton's Cherokee teacher also told him why man must ask the spirit of an animal to forgive him for killing it. He was taught that the name for the Cherokee before the coming of the white man was Ani-Yuwiya, the "Principal People." All others were just Ani-Yuwuyu, "People." This upset the white Christians from Europe, who believed they were the chosen people of God. They refused to call the Cherokee Ani-Yuwiya, using instead a corrupted Choctaw term Chiluk-ki, "People of the Cave Country." Among the whites the word had eventually become "Cherokee," but the Cherokee called themselves Ani-Tsalagi, which had no literal translation.

It upset the Christian missionaries for the old ones to teach these stories of the Cherokee, but Milton loved all of them. When a white teacher had beaten him for repeating some of the old Cherokee stories at school, his Cherokee grandfather, his father's father, had gone to the white teacher and cut off his ear. People did not whip or beat a child of the Cherokee. His grandfather, old Pathkiller, hid in the mountains for two years before he could come back to their town. It was his mother's father, a Hicks, who made it possible for him to return.

"The Broom," chief of Tamotley and later founder and chief of Broom's Town in Georgia, was father of Nayehi, who married Nathan Hicks. Many of her family could speak and write several languages. They were educated beyond most of the white men and women of Georgia. Many of the Cherokee were educated, owned property, and some had become Christians. Instead of placing them in higher esteem with the white people, this had caused jealousy and the red people were considered "uppity red trash." Such illiterate backwoodsmen as Milton had left dead in Nacogdoches were never going to accept the fact that heathen Indians could be more educated and more intelligent than they. And the United States was full of such men.

Milton had learned and accepted those of the white man's

teachings he wanted and quickly forgot the rest. He refused to accept the white man's religion, not understanding it at all. The white man's religion had good rules to live by, but it was a weak religion in his eyes. This religion had not caused white men to live by its teachings. What angered Milton most was the white man's continuous arguing about God and who he did and did not listen to.

He became a warrior of the old school, becoming less and less impressed with the white man's way of making a living. His grandfather, the old chief, could not get Milton to take an active part in leading the young men down the path of the white man. Milton liked the teachings of his other grandfather, and liked being a warrior best of all, even though the need for warriors was becoming a thing of the past.

It was with pleasure that he, along with most other Cherokee warriors, had joined General Andrew Jackson to fight an old traditional enemy of the Cherokee, the Ani-Kusa, as the Cherokee called the Creeks. He and the other Cherokee did not join to fight the War of 1812 because they were patriotic Americans. They joined because they were warriors and could join a fight the white man would not condemn them for.

It was getting hard for a warrior to find a good fight in the new country called the United States. When the combined forces of the Americans and the Cherokee had vanquished the Red Sticks of the Creeks, most of the Cherokee had returned to their beloved mountain homes. A few could not bring themselves to go back and be "good Indians." Milton and a few others had stayed with Jackson and fought in the Battle of New Orleans.

Jackson had been Milton's hero as far as white men went. But his respect for Jackson had turned after he became president. Milton's anger and sadness for what Jackson was saying about taking all southeastern Indians' land turned to hate with passage of the United States Indian Removal Bill of 1830. Jackson had spoken out of both sides of his mouth to get Indians to help him. To the red man he had spoken of honor and respect. To the white man he spoke of desire for Indian land. Jackson had been called "Sharp Knife" and "The Arrow Point" by the Cherokee. From 1830 on, the Cherokee would call him "The Chicken Snake."

When the War of 1812 ended, Milton made a trip to see his family. But wanderlust had taken hold of him. The place his family lived in was not their old traditional home. None of his grandfathers had been buried in southern Tennessee. The sacred fire of his town had been extinguished and he felt there were no Cherokee sacred things left to hold him.

He returned to New Orleans and joined three army friends to start a transportation company that rafted supplies up the Mississippi to be sold to settlers and traders. On their return trip down the river, they brought the settlers' trade goods to New Orleans. Milton's job was to his liking. He kept the crew in fresh meat and scouted ahead along the riverbanks on the lookout for river pirates. Run-ins with pirates were the most satisfying part of the adventure, for when it came to making war, he was Cherokee through and through.

His Cherokee ancestors had been at continuous war for centuries because of their love of battle. When the Europeans had first encountered the Cherokee, they called them the Spartans of the New World. A Cherokee mother would rather have seen her son brought home on a shield than in disgrace as a live coward. Cherokee women were also like the ancient Amazon women of myth. They would take up the war ax and the bow and arrow to fight alongside their men. Women who did this were called members of the Longhair Society. His mother's mother and many women of the older generation had been members of the Longhair Society. With blood of such ancestors as these flowing through his veins, a good fight for Milton was like nectar to the gods.

After the joy of adventure on the river had worn off, he had gone in search of more excitement. In New Orleans he had seen an old army captain of the War of 1812 named Britton "Britt" Bailey. Britt told Milton that he had been thinking of going across the Sabine River to a new country, a land in Mexico the Spanish called Tejas. Milton had been thinking of this country. The Spanish were having problems with the people of Mexico, who wanted their independence. The Spanish were opening up their eastern territory to American and other foreign settlers in hopes that the influx of Anglos would squelch the talk of open rebellion by the Mexicans. Milton knew that whenever revolution was discussed, armed conflict was not far behind. There might indeed be an adventure, he hoped, in this land called Tejas. Milton did not want their land, but it looked like the country where the next fight was going to be.

The breed had listened intently to Britt, then he had told the three friends that it was time for him to move on. He became one of the first Americans to come to Texas to stay. Britt Bailey also came the following year with a Spanish land grant. Britt and his family established a plantation near the lower Brazos River. It was to this same area that Stephen Austin brought his American settlers four years later.

Milton became a citizen of this new country, but without official papers. He never did manage to legally accept Catholicism, which was a requirement by both Spain and later Mexico. It did not matter to him whether he declared for the Roman Catholic church or any other religion. One was as good as another to him. He also did not consider it to be important whether he was called a Spanish citizen, a Mexican citizen, or a United States citizen. He was still a breed Cherokee no matter what his citizenship.

He looked at the forest around him as he rode. Much of it was like his old homeland, with many pine trees, hardwood trees, forest animals, and flowing creeks. But the little hills were only slight rises in the land and nothing like the mountains where he had been brought up as a boy. The countryside around him was beautiful this time of year. The forest floor was covered with early summer flowers that cast a multitude of beautiful colors in the afternoon sun. The bluebonnets, an early spring flower, called *el conejo*, "the rabbit," by the Mexicans, had begun to wither away and turn to seed. There were many other flowers to take their place in beautifying Grandmother Earth. Butterflies and bees flew among the floral scenery of buttercups, daisies, and asters. This warrior who would go into battle to kill or be killed, this mixed blood, not too far removed from what the whites called "savagery," was also a man close to nature and noticed these things. He was a man who loved the beauty Asgaya Galulati had placed upon this earth for man to enjoy.

A sudden noise in the forest to his left caused the big man to cock his rifle in readiness. A yearling deer ran across a small open meadow, bucking and kicking up its heels at every jump. While grazing, the young deer had disturbed a working bee feeding on the nectar of a flower. The bee had retaliated with the weapon with which nature had provided it, a stinger at the end of its tail that would be painful to any foe. The little maker of honey had risen high above the flowers and grass to see if it could find that thing that had interrupted its work. It had seen movement, and the target had been the hip of the young deer.

Milton gave one of his rare belly laughs.

A mile from the Neches River Milton passed close to the mound of an older people. A mound on his left loomed against the dark sky. The Indians in the area could not tell him where these people who had built this mound had come from, where they had gone, or when they had left. He was sure the ancient ones had used the mounds as burial grounds and as a sanctuary for speaking to the Great One. These ancient ones were not favored by the Giver and Taker of Breath like the Cherokee, who had been given lofty peaks in their native land to go upon to pray to the Great Creative Being.

Milton was religious in his own way, the confused way of an American Indian in transition from his belief as it collided with the religion of a stronger people. He loved the high mountains as his base to talk to the Great Creator.

He had missed three days of school when he was a boy because he had gone upon the mountaintop to speak with the Great One. The white teacher did not understand that it was something he had to do. Was he not Cherokee? That should have explained everything. The white teacher had flogged him for speaking blasphemy. His father had flogged the teacher and run the white man out of the Cherokee nation. Another white schoolmaster was lost to the Cherokee, and another member of his family had to go into hiding.

White men could not understand that the American Indian lived every day with his religion. Everything he did was regulated by a religious law. A ritualistic ceremony brought a man into this world and a ritualistic ceremony sent his soul upon an unknown journey from this life. Ritualistic religious ceremonies were demanded of every Cherokee for nearly every undertaking—whether it was the long black drink ceremony or the simple act of a hunter asking quietly under his breath that a brother animal's soul forgive him for killing its little brother for food.

The educated man of the forest shook his head at the mound of mystery and continued to ride. For this man who had more education than the average man and was more intelligent than most, religion was still a perplexing problem.

This was the makeup of the man Milton Hicks.

Chapter Three

Milton crossed the Neches River after the sun had set. He did not bother to call the man who ran the ferry. He rode south down the river a short piece and crossed at a point he knew. Then he rode back north to the road and the campgrounds that everyone used. He would spend the night near the grounds. Milton would make camp well off the trail. It was not safe to sleep near the trail around white men. They rambled around at all hours of the night and could easily step on you in the dark with their horses. The most dangerous thing was for them to mistake you for a "wild" Indian, ready to do them harm. If that happened, no matter if you were sleeping, being near them was excuse enough. Many men, red and white, had been shot in their blankets and dubbed a "bandito" when the sun came up.

His instincts alerted him to the presence of other men before he smelled the smoke of their campfire. From the smells of the camp he knew these men were Mexicans. He preferred them to Anglo frontiersmen like those he had left on the store floor back in Nacagdoches.

The smell was strong. A man's food preparation was a signal of who he was. His food also affected his body odor. Milton knew that his own body smell would change the longer he lived among his Mexican friends. And he would stink. Only an Indian who smeared himself with rancid bear grease to keep off the insects of the forest could smell worse than a white man, whether he was Mexican or Anglo. And the white man had a bad habit of not bathing regularly, adding to the stink. The red man bathed with the rising of every sun if there was water handy.

Milton slowed his horse to a walk and made sure he made enough noise to be heard. Some men on guard duty were a little trigger happy at night when they were far from the security of town—even men who were used to the trail.

"*Alto!*" a voice called out in Spanish. The word "halt!" can be understood in any language, especially if it is called out by a nervous man at night in hostile country. Only the towns belonged to the Mexicans. The forests belonged to everyone.

"Who is there?" the voice inquired in Spanish.

Milton halted his horse and sat quietly. "It is Milton Hicks, and I am alone."

"Come forward, slowly!" the voice ordered.

A deep, friendly voice boomed out in the darkness. "Don Milton! Milton Hicks! Ride on in, my friend! Ride in and welcome!"

Milton rode forward until he came to the main campfire. The man who had called to him walked to the edge of the firelight. He was a tall, dark, broad-shouldered man. The light of the fire shone on dark, reddish hair and gray eyes that sparkled as Milton dropped from his horse to return the handshake. This man was Ricardo Alvino Ignacio Hernandez y Guerra, el Aguila. He was called el Aguila, the Eagle, because of his eaglelike beak of a nose and his clear, eagle-sharp eyes. His blood was pure Spanish, his family not having intermarried with Indians like most of the Spanish colonists.

"Milton Hicks, amigo! Come and rest yourself by our fire. Fill your belly with our food and good coffee," Aguila offered.

"*Gracias*, Aguila," Milton stated, gripping the strong hand of the Mexican. He looked around at the large group of men, ever on the lookout for anything amiss, even among friends. He could smell the horses and mules that were kept outside the camp. Aguila was in the transporting business and owned a pack train that carried goods and supplies from San Antonio de Bexar to the eastern outposts of Texas.

Across the fire he looked into the sparkling black eyes of a beautiful young woman. He could see by her carriage and clothes that she belonged to an aristocratic Mexican family. An older woman sitting on a camp stool beside her was no doubt the chaperon, or *acompañante*, as the Mexicans called her. The *acompañante* was a handsome woman in her mid-thirties. A light, four-wheeled carriage and tent were directly behind the two women. They traveled under the protection of honorable men, in rough country.

"I am glad to see you, friend. I am in need of a good scout and maybe you will be of service to us, eh?" Aguila asked Milton.

"Might be," Milton stated, noncommittal. "You going to de Bexar?"

"Sí! Straight through and no stops," Aguila told him. Then a broad grin crossed his face. "Ah, amigo, I must say we are returning with the flower of all Tejas. No, of all Mexico! This beautiful lady is Senorita Alicia Juanita Rodriguez. She has been visiting her sister in Nacogdoches and is returning to San Antonio. Senorita, this big Anglo-Yankee is Milton Hicks, the best Indian fighter, scout, hunter, and horseman to come to this part of Mexico from Yanqui country."

"Senorita," Milton greeted her.

"Senor Hicks," Alicia said in a soft, firm voice, politely dropping her eyes.

"And this hawk-eye of a woman with her is her aunt and *acompañante*, Senora Luz Lopez," Aguila said, introducing them.

"You know it is senorita, not senora," Senorita Lopez said coldly to Aguila. She smiled at Milton. "Welcome, senor."

Milton nodded and turned to his Mexican friend, never much for words and always to the point. "What is your worry? There are many of you in this party."

"Ah, you have not heard? Some Indians are on the warpath," Aguila told Milton. There was an extra twinkle of merriment in his eyes. Then he grinned broadly. "I think maybe our red brothers are getting angry again because their white brothers keep taking their land."

"They should not be angry in this part of Texas. The Mexican government treats the Indian with honor," Milton said.

"Ah, that is true—for this part of Texas, that is. But the Anglo settlers do not treat the red man so well," replied Aguila.

"Still, the Indians in East Texas will not bother a Mexican group," Milton told him.

That was in all truth the case. It seemed that wherever white men gathered, they had the enmity of all Indians in a short time. A Mexican could travel through the eastern part of Texas with little fear of the Indians, but that same Mexican would face a horrible death if he traveled into the plains of West Texas. The Comanche and Kiowa Indians hated the Spanish and Mexican with a passion that had been well earned.

"It would make the ladies feel so much safer if such an experienced man as you rode with us," Aguila informed him.

Milton smiled inwardly. In all probability the "Indian trouble" was for the benefit of the ladies. He had not heard of any uprisings among the Caddo tribes, which were dominant in the eastern part of Texas, and if there was any trouble, he would have heard of it long before most whites. But there was nothing that would help a romance along more than a possible life-and-death struggle.

"We will pay you well, senor," Alicia put in.

Aguila winced openly, closed his eyes, groaned inwardly and looked up at the dark sky. *Alicia, you are a beautiful woman, but a woman nonetheless,* he thought.

One did not ask a proud man such as Milton Hicks for a personal favor and then offer to pay him money for that service. It was an insult—a slap in the face. It was an affront to his manhood.

Milton ignored the woman. "The Indians around here are at peace. I have heard of no trouble of late."

"Oh, I am not worried for myself or my men, amigo," Aguila said, sidestepping the statement. "But for this beautiful flower and her aunt. I would hate to go to the young lady's father, who is a very powerful man, with hat in hand and say, 'Senor, as we all know, the Indians of East Texas are at peace and are few in number, so I do not take extra care when I hear they are on the warpath. One day, one little arrow he let fly into our camp. Senor, do you know where that one little arrow hit? It hit in the pretty white throat of our beautiful little Senorita Alicia Juanita Rodriquez.' No, amigo. Before I go to face that man, I would leave the country. Maybe even go to that heathen Protestant land of the Anglos, the United States."

Milton continued to smile inwardly. The young Alicia and her aunt were women of the brush country south of San Antonio de Bexar. That was the land of the Comanche, Kiowa, and Lipan Apache. These women did not fear the wilds, and there was nothing in their expressions now to indicate that they feared an Indian attack. Aguila was really laying it on thick for the benefit of the ladies, but they were not overly impressed. Milton knew this tall, slender man feared little himself. But Aguila was a friend who had asked for his help, and big Milton Hicks was not one to turn down such a friend.

After all, who was he to question what was right or wrong for a man to do when it came to the affairs of the heart? Could he not use the threat of an Indian attack to gain inroads into the lady's heart? For his friend was having an affair of the heart.

"All right. I will scout for you," Milton told him.

"Good! Good! Now maybe we will be safe. When the Indians hear that the great warrior Milton Hicks is riding with us, their hearts will melt from fear and they will go to attack easier game. These men I have with me are nothing but poor mestizos. Half-breeds." Aguila smiled broadly, his white teeth flashing in the firelight. "It is a sad thing, amigo, when good Spanish people mix their blood with Indians. It does bad things to them. They become lazy and drunkards."

Aguila eyed a heavyset man who walked up to the fire, a twinkle in his eye. It was obvious that Aguila was talking for the benefit of the man. He continued, "Sí, amigo, they become

fat and lazy, many of these mestizos. And they fear everything. They cannot even go to the bushes alone when it is
dark, they have so much fear."

"Ah! Everything? Everything but skinny little pompous
Spaniards," the heavy man, Pancho Amador, roared as if he
were angry. The short, heavy man of large girth was the right
hand of Aguila's operation, as he had been for Aguila's father.
Aguila's father had been killed a number of years earlier by
bandits. His mother had died the following year of typhus,
leaving the twelve-year-old without a family. Pancho had
taken in the young orphan and run the business until Aguila
became old enough to take over. They had expanded the operation into a good-size firm. The two men were inseparable.
And the heavy, black-eyed man, Pancho Amador, was far from
being weak of heart. "Ah, we have Senor Milton Hicks here to
honor our camp. Don Milton, you are always a welcome
sight."

"It is good to see you, Pancho," Milton said as he returned
the heavy man's powerful handshake. "You are a good man to
meet on the trail."

"Oh, by the Blessed Virgin Mother, don't give the old man
such praise," Aguila said with a mock groan. "He is hard
enough to live with as it is. Now his head will become as large
as that great belly of his."

Pancho grinned. "This *panza grande* is my pride, and that of
Mama's also. We are the true Mexican, a complete new race of
people. While you, the Spanish, are of the old and worn. We
like a little meat on our bones. More so on our women, for
comfort's sake."

He turned to the two ladies and bowed, "Your pardon, senoritas."

"Ha, ha!" Aguila gave a dry laugh.

"Ah, you must be hungry," Pancho said to Milton. "Lupe!
Lupe!"

"He is behind you," Aguila said with a smile.

"Ho! There you are," Pancho said, knowing the old man
could not hear him. Pancho walked up to the frail-looking

little man, bent down close to his ear and roared, "We have a friend who has ridden into our camp and is hungry!"

"Eh?" the little wisp of a gray man called back, using the same loud voice everyone used with him. Evidently he thought the entire world was as deaf as he.

"Why don't you get a horn for the deaf so we won't have to yell so loud to make you hear us, old man!" Pancho yelled at the top of his voice.

"Because, Pancho Amador, I would look the fool having such an ungodly-looking thing hanging from around my neck," the old man called back. "And another important thing . . ."

Pancho waited, and when the old man didn't continue, he asked, "And what very important thing?"

"There is little if anything said in this world I wish to hear," Lupe giggled. "See, yes! Hear, no!"

"We still have a man in need of some food?" Pancho informed him.

"The kitchen is closed," Lupe told him.

"This is for a friend! He is hungry!" Pancho returned, getting tired of the conversation.

"What friend?" the little man asked. He was not impressed by position and rank. A good trail cook was next to impossible to find, and they all knew this fact. Besides, the old man had worked for Aguila's father and was a member of the select few in the group.

"That friend! Don Milton," Pancho roared in Lupe's ear.

"Oh! Don Milton! Why didn't you say so," Lupe said, acting as if he had just noticed Milton. "It is always good to feed a man who brings fresh meat into camp."

Lupe did not offer to shake hands with Milton. Milton had never seen the dried-up little man shake hands with anyone. The old man's wrists were as small as a child's, and he didn't weigh much over ninety pounds. But he had strength. That was evident from the fact that he was a trail cook, and had been for fifty years. Many men had broken under the physical strain of being a trail cook.

Milton walked over to the fire and accepted a tin cup of coffee and a plate of tortillas, beans, and deer meat. He left the hot peppers for the Mexicans. For dessert he had some parched corn, washed down by more hot, black coffee.

The tall man was not overjoyed to be traveling with so many people, but even a wild frontiersman had a little romance in his soul. What better man could he help in the furtherance of a love affair than his young friend Aguila? If there was interference by Indians, which he doubted, it could turn into an interesting trip.

Chapter Four

The next three days were spent in the heavy timber forest of pine and other trees of hard and soft wood. The thickest stands of underbrush were along the rivers and creeks. To those who did not have the eyes of the hunter or woodsman, the pine forest had a monotonous sameness. The average man missed the small squirrel that ran up a pecan tree to peer around its trunk and watch these strange-looking creatures pass, its bushy tail poised, motionless, and not even its little nose giving a twitch. And he would miss the small bandit of the forest with a black mask about its eyes, the raccoon, or *mapache*, as the Mexicans called the animal, sitting on a limb watching the procession pass.

Milton was not the only one to see the animals of the forest as they passed. The scouts for the mule train also observed all that was taking place around them. These men were experts at their job and had spent their lives scouting between the interior of Mexico and its far-flung frontier outposts. For the most part these men were either part or full-blood Indians, and experts of both forest and plains. Having Indians from the plains and the woodlands, Aguila used both to his advantage. It was a well-balanced group of men who worked for the Eagle.

The scouts rode as a relaxed group, yet they were ever ready for the unexpected. Milton smiled slightly. He did not ask these men if they had heard of any Indian uprisings. Their actions spoke for themselves.

A boring trip was made tolerable for the big man by the beautiful Alicia. There was a quick, friendly attraction between the beautiful Mexican lady and this natural-born loner.

Alicia was pure, highborn Spanish, not of the European peasant stock that would leave her squat, dumpy, and splayfooted by middle age. This slim woman had fair skin, silky black hair, and lively blue eyes that revealed the delightful, fun-loving inner person she concealed from the world.

It was to Milton that Alicia chose to reveal some of her inner life. He smiled and shook his head to himself, thinking of the happiness she would give the man of her choice. And the trouble, for she was not a submissive woman. But the joy she would give would never be given to Milton Hicks. Not only was he twice her age—which meant little to Mexicans—but, most of all, he was a rough, half-breed frontiersman, which did mean something to Mexicans of her class. He was a well-educated and well-read man, it was true. In all probability he had more formal education than any of the young men she would marry. But the young Mexican woman was in a class of which he would never be a part. She belonged to the political and landed gentry of Mexico, untouchable by his type in every society and even more so there. Only a few with luck, like Jim Bowie, could break that social barrier. Still, he did enjoy her company, which said much for her, for there were few who could hold his interest.

The light carriage Alicia and her aunt used for transportation was easily pulled over the rough road, but the springless vehicle was also rough on its passengers. Alicia spent much of her time walking or riding horseback; she was a woman of the rancho and rode well. She gave a secretive smile to Pancho on occasion. But when she was not talking with Milton, she remained aloof and neither rode nor walked with any of the other men. When the party camped at night, she sat apart from the rest of the group and went to her blankets with barely more than a civil "Good night."

Aguila looked hungrily after the young woman and a hurt expression came over his face whenever she rebuked his advances. The look in the young woman's eyes made Milton smile outwardly. The big breed knew what Aguila would have given an arm to know. He was winning ground.

The handsome young Aguila was beside himself because of the beautiful Alicia's cold shoulder. He had been sure that a long trip through hostile country would be enough to start an affair. Yet nothing had come of his planning and maneuvering. His disappointment was so obvious that the men laughed at him behind their hands. Big Pancho Amador laughed openly. He knew his Aguila well. It was time this handsome peacock found a young woman who would not come running when he snapped his fingers. It would help him to appreciate and respect the opposite sex more. Yet the heavyset man was all for his young friend and hated to see him suffer.

A little more than a day from San Antonio de Bexar the pack train left the forest of East Texas and started into the open country of low hills and tall grass. Milton now began to scout ahead of the caravan with extra care. He was not worried about the Waco and Tawakoni as they were at peace with the Mexicans at the moment. The caravan was now moving into an area of greater threat. They were in the outer fringes of the land of the Comanche and their cousins, the Kiowa.

He made sure the scouts on night guard were armed with extra alertness on this last night before reaching de Bexar. He rode into camp as the sun was setting. It was as beautiful as a sunset can be in Texas. He unsaddled his horse and was rubbing the animal down when Alicia walked up to him.

"We seem to have avoided any Caddo who were after Mexican scalps," she said with a devilish smile.

"Sí, senorita," he agreed. From her smile, he knew she had known there were no Indian uprisings.

"It looks like your talents have been wasted," she told him.

"Sí, senorita." He could tell from the tone of her voice that she was laughing inside. The smile he reserved for his inner self broadened.

"You have never said, but do you have a family in de Bexar?" she asked.

"No, senorita."

"You are as I suspected from the start. You are a man who does not want a rope around his neck with the weight of a woman hanging from it. You are a man who likes to move around, eh?" she asked with a knowing smile.

"Could be."

"You Anglos are not the only ones who have men such as you. We Spanish have more than our share," she informed him.

"This I know. All peoples have them," he agreed.

"Do you never wish to own property and have a family?" she was so bold as to ask.

Milton stopped brushing his horse and looked at her, showing no emotion. "No man can own land. God has given land for man to live upon and gather its fruits for his benefit. Only a fool can say he owns God's land."

This was stated in a matter-of-fact manner that allowed no opposition or discussion. Alicia did not bother to tell him that her father owned land yet she did not consider him a fool. This was not a man you disagreed with on matters of which he took a definite stand. Not that he would ever speak harshly to her or offer physical harm or look upon her with scorn. But in his quiet way and easy manner, he would make her feel the fool. To this man God and nature and all living creatures were one and the same. How can man own something that is part of himself? Milton would never kill out of lust or desire for another's personal possessions, and he would certainly never steal. To kill out of necessity or on occasion out of revenge was part of life and an accepted thing to him; this was part of the nature of things.

She watched the broad-shouldered man rub down his horse, his huge hands moving swiftly and with affection, for this animal bore his weight in their travels and shared his companionship and solitude.

"Pancho tells me that you are a friend of Jim Bowie," she said.

"Yes."

"Will you go see him and his new wife?" Alicia asked.

"No."

"Like many of our conversations, this one is also one-sided," she told him.

He smiled but remained silent, continuing to brush his horse.

"This is something!" she exclaimed in mock exasperation. "I can't get you to talk half the time and I can't get Aguila to keep quiet!"

"The problems of being a beautiful woman. You make some men tongue-tied and others loose in the head, their tongues wagging on and on," he informed her, looking up from his work.

"All except the big Yanqui, Milton Hicks. Your tongue is neither tied nor loosened by a woman, is it?" she asked.

Again he smiled, but said nothing.

Alicia cocked her head to one side and looked at him. She shook her head slightly, the gold from the last rays of the sun sparkling in her dark hair. "No, a woman would never make you tongue-tied or loose-tongued. You would be good to your woman as long as you were around, but none will ever be able to hold you, Milton Hicks. While you were with her, she would be happy and in a heaven of her own. Then one fine morning in that quiet, easy way of yours, you would saddle your horse and ride off in search of something else. Do you know what you are searching for?"

"No, I do not know what I am searching for. I don't even know if I would know I had found it if it reached up and slapped me in the face." He paused. He had done something he seldom did with anyone. He had revealed some of his inner self. "No, Alicia, I know not for what I search. I do not wish to find anything, and I will not allow anything to be found. It's as simple as that."

She stood a moment, aware of the rare gift he had given her. Not many such as he would ever share even a small part of themselves with anyone. This would in all probability be the one and only occasion, but it would always be a bond between them.

"You have broken many women's hearts in the past and you

will do so again, Don Milton," she said lightly. She started to walk away but turned back to face him. "We women had better stick to men like Aguila. He is a brave man and a strong man among men, but he is the type to obey the bridle and spur of the right woman."

She turned and walked back to camp. When she arrived, she placed her stool well away from the rest of the group. Milton smiled. His young friend had better be prepared to be broken to ride. Most men never knew when the breaking began, so painless was the operation.

Aguila sat on a keg, brooding over a cup of coffee. He motioned Milton to another keg beside him. The tall breed sat down with his tin plate of meat, beans, and tortillas. He looked at Aguila. The young Mexican sat in silence.

"Hey, amigo, what do I do about the beautiful senorita who is slowly driving me loco? She will not give me the time of day. She will talk only to you and Pancho. Of you both, I am jealous," Aguila told his friend in a strained voice.

Milton looked at Aguila, and this time he did not smile at his young friend. Aguila was suffering, indeed. It was not a thing he himself would do. No woman was worth such a thing. Some men were of that nature, but not he. Yet who was he to either condemn or approve?

"I am twice her age and Pancho is even older," Milton told him. "Besides, we are your friends."

This time Milton did smile.

"That is true. But age does not make any difference where the heart is concerned. I do not know what or where her heart lies. Horror of horrors if she does not talk to me because she does not find I am worthy," Aguila groaned. "I am not old. I have only twenty-five years—eight years her senior. Does she wish someone who is younger? Does she like little boys—not the big, tough macho men of the world?"

There was such despair in Aguila's voice. He looked so ludicrous that Milton had to suppress an open smile. The big man never thought he would see the day el Aguila would be re-

duced to behaving like a lovesick schoolboy. He started to tell
his friend that the lady was already captured but held his
tongue. It was none of his business, and Alicia should be the
one to make her own move. It would be a much sweeter capture for both of them.

Milton continued to eat in silence.

If Alicia ever planned to approach the lovesick man, she
gave no sign of it for the rest of the trip. Yet everyone except
Aguila knew that she would approach him sooner or later.
Milton hoped Aguila would have sense enough to know that
she was asking to be captured when the right time came. Both
of the young people were vain and self-serving in many ways,
and used to having their own way. They were always the center of things. It would be a twist of fate if Aguila thought the
young woman of his dreams was only making fun of him
when she suddenly showed open interest.

Pancho watched the two young people and knew that he
was about to gain another daughter. Mama would be happy.
They had only eight daughters. But most of all it would keep
their Aguila from the cantinas, and Mama wouldn't have to
burn so many candles at the altar.

Everyone else knew of Aguila's fate. Everyone except the
victim himself.

Chapter Five

The pack train arrived in the old Spanish town of cathedrals late in the afternoon. They had reached their destination. The mission town of San Antonio de Bexar was referred to more and more as simply San Antonio. Although it had a population of little more than 3,000, in this isolated part of Mexico it was considered a city.

From a small rise at the northeast section of town, Milton could see the four Franciscan missions to the south. The oldest, over 114 years old, was La Purisima Concepción de Acuma. Two years its junior was San José y San Miguel de Aguayo. The latter was considered to be the most beautiful of all the missions in North America. Its design was simple, all ornaments were made with crude tools by local Indians, and raw materials were gathered from the surrounding area. The other two missions were built at the same time, in 1731. They were San Juan Capistrano and San Francisco de la Espanda, with its rare fortified tower. In the center of town was the San Fernando Cathedral. The large iron cross on top of its tower marked the exact location for the center of town.

The largest private dwelling was the governor's palace, which had housed the royal governor during Spanish colonial days. Now that the territory was considered the state of Coahuila-Texas combined, the vice-governor lived there. The present vice-governor was Don Juan Martin Beramendi. He was also the father-in-law of Milton's friend Jim Bowie. San Antonio had been reduced to an administrative center for the area, the capitol being located in Saltillo.

Around the governor's palace was La Villita, the "Little Village," which was built by soldiers and their families after the founding of the missions. The village of the soldiers and their families had grown in size over the years since it was first started in 1718. It was now surrounded by the new buildings of many latecomers. All were made in the traditional adobe, flat-roofed style that had become a symbol of Spanish settlement in the New World.

Across the street was the military plaza, where more than one execution had been held during Spanish rule. Soldiers' barracks were immediately behind the square. Nearby was the old, abandoned mission fort called Mission San Antonio de Valero, built in 1744. When it became a military barracks, it was renamed El Alamo, after the town of Alamo de Parras in Mexico.

The San Antonio River made its twisting, switchback way through the settlement. Some said that it had an Indian name that meant "drunken-old-man-going-home-at-night." If so, it had to be a recent name, for the Indians of the area had nothing to make them drunk until the white man came with his beer, wine, and rum.

Milton looked at the growing size of the town. There were not more than 7,000 white people in all of Texas when Mexico won its independence from Spain in 1821. But there were more and more whites coming in from the United States. There would now be more than 7,000 white people in San Antonio and Brazoria alone. Brazoria was the main town of Austin's settlement along the Río Brazos. Texas was being overrun by what the red man called the "white, Christian plague."

The entire populace of San Antonio de Bexar, and all of their dogs, ran out to meet the caravan. San Antonio was isolated from the rest of the state as well as from the rest of the country. It was not every day something as important as a pack train came to town to break the monotony and bring news from the outside world. Wives and children ran to greet the men. Ladies of the evening ran to meet those in need of a woman. There would be much singing and dancing in all the cantinas tonight. And a little drinking. Men, long on the trail, would receive their pay. Women lined up to receive the benefits of the men's labors, be they wives or ladies of the evening.

The vice-governor, Don Beramendi, and the alcalde, Don Ramón Musquiz, along with Colonel Pablo Ruiz, came out to greet them. All were anxious for news from the troublesome town of Nacogdoches and the eastern frontier. News kept filtering down from the eastern outposts that more and more Anglo-Americans were coming across the border in defiance of the new Mexican law. Many of these men were the type that were not welcome in Mexico because of their mean manner and their tendency toward outlawry. They would never become law-abiding citizens of Mexico. Why couldn't the Yanquis coming into Mexico be an honorable group like those in Austin's colony? Of course, the members of that colony were hand-chosen by Austin.

The central government of Mexico could not send more troops to protect the borders from land-hungry border jumpers. The new president, Bustamante, had overthrown the old regime with the aid of the hero of the war for Mexican independence from Spain, General Antonio López de Santa Anna. Many revolutions that are gained by the gun must also be held by the gun. Santa Anna, Bustamante's old comrade-in-arms, was now conspiring to overthrow him. The president could not send troops to protect the frontiers of Mexico because he needed to keep them close to Mexico City. None of the soldiers loyal to Santa Anna would go to the frontiers and desert the general. So the borders of Mexico were only thinly guarded by soldiers whose loyalty to either party was uncertain.

This was only politics, which held little or no interest for Milton Hicks. He was in search of a hot bath and something to eat. Something soft to lay his head upon would also be of interest later in the evening.

Politics was also of no interest to young Aguila. His only interest at the moment was held by one Senorita Alicia Juanita Rodriguez of the Hacienda de la Cepillo de Espinas, the

"Ranch of the Brush of Thorns." The hacienda was located some forty miles southwest of San Antonio in an area that could in truth be called a brush of thorns, the true chaparral area of Texas.

Aguila left Pancho to answer all the silly questions about illegal Yanquis and the political intrigues of Mexico. He didn't care which army officer leaned toward Bustamante or which leaned in favor of General Santa Anna. When the fight came, he would choose and do his duty to God, flag, and country.

There were times when he became disgusted with the people of his country. It seemed that everyone in Mexico thrived on political intrigue instead of working toward a settled government. It was said by men of other countries, even by those Yanquis of the United States, that the Mexican constitution of 1824 was one of the most ideal constitutions ever written. Yet there was revolution after revolution in his country. Without stability, the problems of his people and country would never be solved. This was not the way to build a nation. Even a man less knowledgeable than he could understand that. Would these senseless revolutions and counterrevolutions never cease?

Aguila quickly forgot about his country's problems and went in search of more pleasant things, however. He knocked on the door of Antonio Domingo Gregory Alvarez de Córdoba, a man who had powerful connections here in Mexico and in the old mother country, Spain. Don Antonio was a very mysterious man and had been involved in every revolution and attempted revolution or other intrigue in Mexico. When the Yanqui McGee formed an army of Americans and crossed the border of Mexico to aid the Mexicans in their first try for independence in the Revolution of 1810, Cordoba aided the Mexicans in their fight for freedom. When the Spanish crushed the rebelling Mexicans in the Battle of Medina a few miles west of de Bexar, Cordoba easily switched from the revolutionary side to the side of the Spanish government. He did so without arousing the anger of either faction. It was also said that he had some dealings with the American filibusterer, Dr. James Long.

When Mexico did win its independence from Spain in 1824, there he was arranging everything for both sides. Aguila did not know who the man was or what his business was, but he was a friend of Alicia's and had also been a friend of Aguila's father for many years. His father had given him one piece of advice many years ago, and that was never to cross Don Antonio.

A servant answered the door and led Aguila into the presence of Dona Josefa, Don Antonio's wife. With her was a worried Alicia and Tia Luz. Tia Luz was seated, fanning herself vigorously. It was much hotter here in San Antonio than it had been in Nacogdoches.

"Oh, Aguila!" Alicia exclaimed as she came to meet him. "My father and my brothers! None of them are here to meet me!"

"I am sorry," Aguila said, at a loss what else to say.

"If you will pardon me," Dona Josefa said, and left the room.

Neither of the young couple saw her leave.

"Did you expect them to be here waiting for you?" asked Aguila.

"Of course I expected them!" exclaimed Alicia.

"No, I mean today. Could it not be that they will arrive tonight or tomorrow?" he asked, still unable to understand her concern.

"No, today. They were to be here today," Alicia told him. "Maybe, if you will, you can ride out and see what is wrong or take us with you."

"Maybe they just forgot that it was today," he said, smiling at her.

"What!" she exclaimed, as if it was incredible for anyone to think such a thing.

"You know." His voice became weak and confused at her violent reaction. "Maybe they were busy and forgot what day it is."

"My father is not a forgetful peon. He would never forget such a thing. Just because you are one to run around wildly in search of yourself doesn't mean everyone in the world is like that! Do you think my father is a bumbling idiot who uses false rumors of possible Indian massacres to try and win the favors of young ladies?" She stamped her foot impatiently.

"I meant no offense. I only thought maybe they would wait until tomorrow to come and get you," Aguila said lamely.

"They should be here today. They would not leave me to wait in town overnight with home so close," she said primly, a cold aloofness coming between them. "They know the date of the arrival of the pack train. Either my father or one of my brothers should be here waiting. We would be prepared to leave early tomorrow before it became hot. If they are not here, then there has been trouble. We live in the brush country where there are bandits and Indians. We do not live safely in town like a bunch of scared, old women. Those Indians are not the tame mission Indians you have here. They are Comanche and Lipan Apache and Kiowa!"

"Yes, I know. I have traveled through that area many times. I am sure that your family has not forgotten you," he said quickly, giving his most winning smile. It had little effect on her. "Luckily I am here to show you our fair city and to be at your service while you await the arrival of your family. *Su servidor.*"

Aguila gave a polite bow.

"*Su servidor?* You, my servant? You show me your fair city? Like I am some farm girl of a peon family who has never been to a city?" she said coldly, a slight rise in her voice. "I, senor, have been instructed in the best schools for young ladies in Mexico City. After living in Mexico City, senor, do you expect me to look upon this small huddle of mud huts as a city? Not only do I not look upon this small village as a fair city, senor, but how dare you be so presumptuous as to think of yourself as having enough social standing to escort me anywhere!"

She turned her back to him.

Aguila stood hat in hand, crushed, his world falling apart.

What had happened? What did he do wrong? He started to protest that he was innocent of any wrongdoing but stopped himself, drawing himself up straight. Never would he bow as a humble peon to anyone. He managed to stammer a *"Buenas tardes"* and stumbled blindly to the door, forgetting to bid Señorita Luz a good afternoon.

Luz watched her niece. She knew why Alicia had reacted so vehemently. She was worried about her family. It was a family of men who spoiled and pampered their women. Alicia knew that her beloved father would have been here himself on her arrival, or sent one of her brothers, if nothing was wrong. Luz also knew that Alicia did not wish to show Aguila her true feelings of love for him at the present. Let him court her in the true manner of the Spanish, then she would gradually show the young man that he was indeed the one of her heart. But Alicia had made a complete fool of herself. She had acted like the spoiled child she was. And she was also experiencing all the pain of a young woman's first love. Ah! The agony of affairs of the heart.

Alicia walked to a window and looked through the Spanish-style barred window and into the courtyard. It was beautiful in all its multicolored floral bloom. The flowers had been carefully planted to form intricate designs. Dona Josefa was an accomplished landscaper. A swift-winged hummingbird darted from flower to flower, its wings beating so rapidly they were nearly invisible. Alicia didn't see this beautiful display of arranged nature. The tears that had sprung so quickly to her eyes blinded her. She was worried about her family. Their ranch was in an isolated area of South Texas, and the bandits and Indians were getting braver now that the state was being stripped of military protection.

And what about Aguila? She stamped her foot in anger, not caring that her aunt was present. She had acted like a silly schoolgirl. She did not really think of San Antonio as a little village of mud hovels. This was her town also, even if she wasn't born here. She was a country girl who had been born and raised on a ranch, not a prim little debutante who must take an afternoon siesta every day and swooned every time she was in danger. And she could also forgo the traditional court-ing of a suitor, for this was Tejas, the frontier, where things happened suddenly and definitely. That was why the peon girls married when they were thirteen or fourteen years old. They grabbed the man they wanted and hung on to him for as long as this hard land would allow.

Oh, this so handsome, strong, intelligent Ricardo Alvino Ignacio Hernandez, called the Eagle, did he not come from a well-respected Spanish family like herself? Just because he had been brought up from childhood by Mexican mestizos didn't mean he was also one. Did he not have his own wealth and good name? It was true that Aguila was not as wealthy and powerful as her landed father. But he would be someday, of that she was certain. He was an enterprising young man and had increased his father's business threefold, so Pancho had told her. With her behind him, he might someday garner more wealth and standing than even the *patrón*, her father.

She twisted her handkerchief in her hands and stamped her foot again.

"You are a vain young fool, my niece," her aunt said quietly.

Alicia wheeled around and shouted, "You should know! You have chased away enough would-be husbands!"

A shocked look came across Luz's face, followed by a hurt expression. Alicia had never talked to her mother's sister in such a manner in all her life, and she, too, was shocked.

Alicia ran to her *tía* and fell to her knees before the seated woman. "Oh, *tía*, *tía*, please forgive this foolish girl who is your niece and loves you!"

The hurt look on Luz's face softened and she took her niece's head into her arms and kissed the top of her head. "Hush, *sobrina*, hush. I know how you feel. I know."

Alicia knew the story of her mother's youngest sister. Luz had once had the love that people are blessed with only once in a lifetime, if at all. It was a love compared with which all others would be of little or no consequence. Shortly before she was to be married, the Revolution of 1824 against Spain began.

Her only true love was an officer loyal to Spain and he had gone to war, begging her not to press him to marry her in such an uncertain time. Wait until the war is over, he told her. He did not wish to leave a young widow behind if fortune failed to smile upon him. He marched off to war, and she saw him for the last time. He was killed in the first weeks of battle.

The grieving young woman had come to Texas nine years earlier to live with her older sister and her family. The ranch was far removed from forced social life. It was now doubtful that the once sweet-hearted Luz would lose the hardness and bitterness that had grown around her mouth and eyes long enough to find a new love. She had found a new life helping her sister care for her children. Caring for another's children was not a fulfilling life, but Luz was convinced that she would never find another to replace her lost love and provide her with children of her own. She had no desire to raise children fathered by a man other than her first love.

"Don't worry, *sobrina,*" she told her niece. "He will not run away. Not this one. The angel Cupid has driven his arrow deep."

Alicia closed her eyes tightly. She prayed that her aunt was right. Oh, she had to be right.

Chapter Six

Milton pushed his way through the crowd. He had no trouble moving people out of his path. His little Indian pony bared its teeth and backed its ears if a stranger came close to him. Everyone gave the war pony and its master a wide avenue to pass through. Milton walked down the street to his favorite place in San Antonio de Bexar, the Cantina del Toro Negro, the "Cantina of the Black Bull." The woman he wanted to visit was also there.

The big breed did like one custom of his white grandfathers' people—that of going to an establishment that served drinks where a man could eat roast duck and tortillas made of cornmeal and listen to music. It was a better custom than his red grandfathers' people had of sitting in the woods and getting crazy drunk, then sleeping off their drunkenness and going home with a hangover to beat their families. Or some would sell more of their meager holdings to buy more of the white man's rotgut whiskey.

The Cherokee had changed since the coming of the white man, and for the most part it was for the worse. Milton was torn between the two races for what they were doing to each other with alcohol, with the red race getting the worst end of the deal.

He liked the custom of drinking and eating in a happy cantina, but he could not do it every night. While the joy lasted, he enjoyed it to the fullest. Those who saw him sitting quietly at a table in the back of the cantina, slowly drinking his tequila, doubted that he was enjoying or taking part in all the festivities around him.

When he walked into the dark, cool interior of the cantina, those who knew him called out a greeting. All of these men were Mexicans he had known since he came to Texas. Milton carried his rifle but not because he thought it would be needed here in de Bexar; this was the place where his lodgings would be. The rifle was to be taken with his other things to an upstairs room that he always used while in town.

"Hey! Look here, amigos! Don Milton has left the forest of the east to visit his friends of de Bexar!" Miguel Gonzalez, the heavy, robust owner of the cantina called. He held out a fat and soft, but strong, hand to Milton.

Milton smiled and a good feeling came over him. He did not care much for town people, but he was now among friends. "Did Lupe have that baby this winter?"

"Oh, sí! She have it. Another boy!" Miguel beamed.

"How many do you have now, Miguel?" Milton asked.

"Boys, or *ninos* of all kinds?" Miguel asked, grinning.

"*Ninos.*"

"We now, my Lupe and me, have nine. Five boys and four girls. Before we get through, we maybe have fifteen, or even more. Not bad for a fat man, eh?" The laugh was from the pit of his huge belly and was infectious.

Milton smiled and shook his head. "I now know how the Indian can win against the white man. All of them should marry Mexicans. In ten years their children would cover the land as thick as the buffalo. In fifty, as thick as the grass!"

"Ah, sí, amigo. But what is a Mexican if he is not Indian? We are not true Spaniards. But, of course, these Indians you talk about, they must also change their religion to the Holy Catholic Church of Rome. The padre, he tells me that God will bless my Lupe and me for making so many Catholics for the church."

"You're making them all right," Milton told him.

"Sí. I think maybe my virility has come from the mixture of my blood, Spanish and Indian." He gave a deep, rumbling belly laugh and rubbed his great stomach fondly. "Maybe some of that strength of manhood came from this great *panza* of mine. It is so huge that I cannot see my *huevos*, but I know they are there. So does my Lupe."

"That may be so, but she also has to be fertile, not just you," Milton told him.

"Oh, sí! That is true. I do not take all the credit. A man should not forget the woman," Miguel said, laughing. "It takes both the flint and the metal to strike the spark."

After much laughter, he called to the rear of the cantina. "Jesús! Maria! Come! *Pronto! Al instante!*"

A young boy of twelve came from the kitchen. His hair and eyes were as black as midnight. A big smile covered his thin face when he saw Milton. The young have an uncanny knack of knowing whether adults truly like them. Milton liked this young boy, and the boy knew that he could be counted as one of the few friends of the tall man. The slender boy prayed to the Virgin Mother that he would grow up to be such a huge man as his father's friend. But he knew that he would probably grow to be the typical size of the average Mexican of mestizo blood—a short, stocky, dark-skinned man like his father. In all probability he would never be more than a cantina owner like his father. Nevertheless, when you are only a twelve-year-old boy, it is easy to dream of what may be. And his dream was to be a giant of a man such as this Milton Hicks.

Jesús' dark-eyed sister Maria followed him. She was thirteen years old and was already developing into a woman. Her full breasts strained against the thin, tight blouse she wore. The young girl would hold her good looks until she was thirty years old, then she would become a squat, plump duplicate of her mother.

Milton could tell by the look in her eyes that she had become aware that she was now a woman. Lupe had better keep an eye on her.

Jesús held out a slim hand to shake Milton's huge one. He no longer ran and hugged the tall man's neck as he had done a few years earlier. He was growing up.

Maria stood on her toes and slyly gave Milton a kiss on both cheeks. She made it a point to rub her young breasts against his arm before she pulled away.

"Maria, take Don Milton's things upstairs," Miguel directed his daughter. He then smiled at Milton. "Velia is upstairs asleep. If she knew you were here, well, she would be down those stairs, BAM, like that!"

"Place my gear against the back wall," Milton told Maria. He handed her the leather pouch with the silver goblet. The others knew that this possession was the most dear to the big man. They knew that it was Milton's personal honor, and honor was above life itself to the tall man. Milton knew that the Mexicans understood his feelings not only for the goblet but for more personal honor far better than did the Anglos.

"I will see Velia later," Milton told Miguel.

"Good! Good! A man must have free time to drink a little and visit with his friends before his woman tries to smother him with her soft arms and affection—and all the other soft things a woman possesses." Miguel gave his booming, infectious laugh. "I will tell her later that you were here. Then run like the scared jack rabbit. The wait will make her into a wild one for when you get back." Then he added for his own personal pleasure and that of his customers, "Tonight, wala! She will make you forget those lonely nights on the trail!"

There was respectful, subdued laughter from the customers.

"Jesús!" boomed Miguel, "Jesús! Take Don Milton's horse to the stall in back. See that he is cared for in the manner Don Milton takes care of his animals."

"I don't think he will give you trouble, Jesús," Milton said to the boy. "He should remember you from the last time. If he will not let you move him, leave him for me."

"Sí, Don Milton," the boy said, running to accomplish his assigned chore.

Milton walked out of the cantina and into the street. The crowd of people who had come out to meet the pack train was beginning to thin. Most of the men would go to their favorite drinking places and drink and talk over the news Aguila and his men had brought from the frontier. Work would be forgotten for the rest of the day. Some were concerned about the Yanquis who were coming in from the United States, and this subject would bring about a few heated discussions. Mostly, they drank and watched the pretty senoritas dance.

After a few drinks with some of his friends Milton returned to the cantina. He needed a bath, and there was also a woman at the cantina to take care of his needs. His manhood demanded that these needs be soothed. His Indian blood demanded that he keep his body clean.

He saw Velia sitting in the back of the cantina when he walked in. She ran to him and, with both arms locked tightly about his neck, pulled his head down and kissed him, much to the enjoyment of the rest of the customers in the cantina. Public display of affection always embarrassed Milton, but he was pleased to be remembered.

Velia was a pretty, olive-skinned, brown-eyed woman in her late twenties. She was one of those lucky people who are blessed with looks that will hold until they are in their fifties. Her skin was firm and smooth, her black hair as fine as silk, and she had a trim body with firm breasts. Of her mixed heritage of Spanish, French and Mescalero Apache blood, Spanish was the most dominant.

She danced in the cantina for her livelihood. If she found favor in a man, he could share her bed—for a price. Very little is free in this world, and she had found long ago that she had what men would pay good money to get. She would charge them all for her favors. All except this big Yanqui. This man would share her bed for free as long as he wished, and no other man in the Mexican state of Tejas would come near her when he was in town. Velia would still dance and laugh and drink with the customers, but no one but Milton would share her bed. She would wish it could last for six months, but she would be lucky if she held him for a week or two. The big man was not one you bridled and broke to the saddle.

"You big donkey, why did you not call me when you came? One yell and I would hear you." She scowled at him. She did not wait for an answer from her closemouthed lover, but turned to lead him to her table. She left him when he was seated, saying, "I'll get you something to eat, big man."

She left, and Miguel brought Milton a mug of beer. Velia returned, followed by Miguel's wife, Lupe.

"Ah, Senor Don Milton, you have come to pay us a visit. Good! Now maybe I will have some deer meat for my kitchen. There is always fresh meat when you are here. These lazy *cabrónes* here will not go to the woods to hunt. They beg off and say they fear the Comanche. Ah! But no! I do not think it is the Comanche they fear! It is the work!"

Lupe was a short, heavyset woman with a strong appearance of Plains Indian blood. Her face was flat and broad, and it looked as if someone had hit her in the nose with one of her heavy frying pans. Her complexion was the color of tobacco juice. Her hips were broad from giving birth to fourteen children, five of whom had died at birth or before they had gained a year of age. The strain of losing her little ones to the diseases of the frontier and the long, hard fourteen- and fifteen-hour workdays showed in her deeply lined face. Still, it had done nothing to daunt her fiery spirit or dull her sharp tongue.

"Now, Mama, you shame your men with such talk," Miguel protested with a large, affectionate grin.

The other men in the cantina smiled also. Everyone in San Antonio loved this woman and knew that she loved them in return. Lupe was one of those rare women who are mothers to the world.

"Ha! You cannot shame this bunch," Lupe returned, slapping Milton fondly on the shoulder. She feared no one, not even this big, tough frontiersman whom everyone else gave such wide berth. Besides, this man was her friend and in his own quiet, barbaric way, he was as fond of her as she of him.

"I am glad you are here," Lupe said, starting back to the kitchen. "Maybe this time you make a little baby so you don't go away again."

She laughed happily at her own humor.

"You dirty-minded old woman," Velia called after her.

But there was no anger in her voice, only the same tone of

affection that had been in Miguel's. Velia loved Lupe with a love that was crossed between that for a mother and an older sister. Lupe had found Velia plying her trade as a prostitute of the streets when Velia was only thirteen years old. The young girl's mother, brothers, and sisters had been killed just outside de Bexar in an Indian raid. Her father, a worthless drunk, had abandoned her and had not been seen in years. Lupe, a young mother with a large and growing brood of her own, took the waif into her own home and Velia had worked in the cantina ever since. As time passed and Velia turned into a woman, the urge to make men happy made her return to what must have been her natural profession, the oldest one. She had talked Lupe and Miguel into letting her move out of the family quarters in the rear of the cantina and upstairs to a room of her own. Lupe crossed herself, went to the San Fernando Cathedral to light candles, cried to the good priest, and returned to the cantina with a resigned acceptance that what will be, will be.

With soldiers stationed a few blocks away, the young woman was never short of business. Because of her beauty, happy disposition, and gentle manner, she could charge a price that was gladly paid by all. The officers and senior sergeants could afford her price more often, but the young soldiers could afford only one trip a month. It was a most satisfying trip for those who went.

Milton finished his meal and drank his second beer. Afterward Velia led him out the back door of the cantina and to a small room at the end of the stable. Inside was the largest wooden tub in San Antonio, perhaps in all of Texas. It was almost full of cold water, and a large iron pot in the yard held hot water. The windows were covered with the skins of animals to make the room into a hot bathhouse like those used by the Cherokee.

His clean pair of corded pants, a new buckskin shirt, and a new pair of moccasins were laid out on a bench. He did not see this woman very often but she knew his habits, and the main thing he wanted when he rode in was a hot bath. A bath in the huge wooden tub came before sex. Milton bathed more than any of the other Anglo frontiersmen Velia knew—even more than the high-class Spaniards. And she made sure she took extra care of her own personal cleanliness as long as he was around.

Jesús and Maria assisted Velia in bringing the hot water from the iron pot and pouring it into the wooden tub. Milton noticed Maria looking closely when she and Jesús were told to leave. She knew that Velia always took a bath with him and scrubbed him down. The look in the young girl's eyes told him that she had become ripe for some young man to pluck. As she closed the door on her way out there was a promise in her look that informed him that she could outdo the older woman.

Milton pulled off his clothes and got into the big tub. Velia watched his superb, physically fit body slowly sink under the hot water. Except for the scars of battle, it was a flawless body of animal strength and litheness. She knew that Milton was part Indian, but the part of his body that was kept from the sun and wind by his clothing was nearly as white as any Anglo's. The sun and other elements had brought out the Indian in him, leaving his face, hands, and neck a hickory-nut brown.

Velia stripped off her clothes and got into the tub. A gasp escaped from between clenched teeth as the hot water covered her body. Both breasts bobbed to the top.

Milton was quiet and reserved in a group of people, and he seemed almost bashful when cornered by a lady. His hard strength could be felt by all in his presence, and his don't-tread-on-me look held them all at a distance. But in the privacy of his family or close friends, or with the woman who shared his bed, the tall man loved a good joke and small play as much as anyone.

He never had the guilty feeling of having an affair with a woman besides his wife. He was not married now, but he had been—to three different women. All of them had been Chero-kee. He had married one when he was a young man back in the "old country." His other two wives had come from Chief

Bowl's tribe in East Texas. He had never married a white
woman in a church wedding, nor would he ever do so. This
caused too much trouble if a man decided he no longer wanted
the woman and it was time to move on. It was a simple matter
for a Cherokee to get a divorce. All the man had to do was
pack his personal things and move out. Or the woman could
set his belongings outside the door.

The couple moved from the bathhouse to Velia's upstairs
room. She flung herself down upon the bed, a pleased smile on
her face. Her man had come to make her happy for a while.
The bed she had was comfortable to most, but after a night or
less, Milton became uncomfortable and felt as if he were lying
on mush. There was no firmness to support his body, and he
seemed to be sinking into the depths of a Louisiana bog. Every
morning Velia woke to find him sleeping on the floor, an arm
under his head for a pillow.

After their passion had been spent, Velia sat up in bed.
"Milton, let us go downstairs and you can drink beer. It has
been dark only a short while and I must sing tonight." Then
she giggled. "Besides, it is a sin to be in bed so early," she
added.

He grunted agreement and got up to dress, glad to get out of
the uncomfortable bed and the small room.

"You go find some of your friends to drink with," she told
him, not wishing to act as if she were trying to hold him
down. "Today the soldiers at the garrison were paid and they
have money to buy tequila. I must go down and dance to bring
them in to spend that money."

He gave another grunt. She did not have to explain her
business to him. And it did not bother him that she danced
and sang for the men in the cantina. She was a partner to share
a bed, not his woman. He would stay for a few days, leave
some money behind to pay his own way, and go in search of
something new. He paid his own way. He was not a kept man.

Chapter Seven

Milton walked along the edge of the dark, dusty street, listening to loud music and laughter from the cantinas. The Mexicans were a happy people and always willing to have a fiesta. There was no better reason to have a fiesta than the return of friends from weeks on the trail. Especially when those friends have just been paid their wages and have plenty of money to keep the wine and tequila flowing.

Two men staggered down the middle of the street, arm in arm, holding each other upright. They greeted Milton boisterously, though none too coherently. Milton recognized both of them as drovers who worked for Aguila. It was going to be a wild night in the sleepy little village of San Antonio de Bexar.

Three other men walked down the middle of the street, one supported by the other two on either side. The sharp-eyed frontiersman could see by their faint outline against the sky that two of the men wore the military hats of the Mexican army. As the trio approached, the coal oil lamps on the front of the old Spanish governor's house cast their lights upon them. Milton saw that the man being supported and carried along by the other two was his friend Aguila. The two soldiers were officers of the garrison.

When Aguila saw Milton he pulled free of his escorts and staggered forward.

"Ah! My friend! My friend of the trail! Come! We must have some wine together!" Aguila turned to the two army officers, tripping and nearly falling. Milton caught him and held him upright.

"*Gracias*, amigo." Then to the two officers, "My friends, you must meet my very good Yanqui friend. We have been friends for a long time, this Yanqui and me. He is Milton Hicks, the best Indian fighter and tracker and scout in all of Tejas. No! In all of Mexico!"

He grabbed Milton's arm to keep himself upright. The officers took note that Aguila dared be so familiar with the tall man. Only a good friend could do so.

Aguila continued, "Amigo, these two, these men of the sword, they are my very good friends. Capitán Medero and Teniente Ybarra."

"Capitán. Teniente," Milton greeted the two officers.

Both men knew Milton Hicks. Every soldier who had served in Texas for the past ten or so years either knew the tall Americano personally or by reputation. They knew him to be a fair man with no mean streak to start trouble. They also knew that if trouble came, they would wish to be on his side. They welcomed him, even if he did make them feel a little uncomfortable at times.

"It has been a long time since we have had the pleasure of your company," Capitán Medero said.

Milton merely shook his head in acknowledgment.

Aguila, still holding Milton's arm with a biting, vicelike grip, looked up at him. His eyes were bloodshot and he had trouble focusing them in the dim light. "Amigo! Amigo! She is like all women! For no reason, they cry. For no reason, they laugh. For no reason, they scream and get angry. Don Milton, my friend, I am lost."

Milton looked down at his friend. Even the strong sometimes whimper when it comes to matters of the heart, he thought. I am glad that I have never been overwhelmed by a woman. The tall man took a firm grip on Aguila's arm and started walking toward a cantina. The two officers followed.

"No, my friend, you are not lost. When you take your pack train out again, then you will find yourself. But first we must have some wine. Then get you to bed," Milton advised.

Milton looked back over his shoulder and saw the Mexican midget who had been watching them from a distance while they talked. He followed them in a carriage. His size had been dwarfed by nature, but he did not have the deformed legs, short arms, and normal-size head on a small body that were common to most midgets Milton had seen; he was a miniature of a handsome grown man.

Milton motioned for Medero to come up alongside. "Who is that little one following us? I have not seen him before."

Medero looked back. "Ah, that is Angel. When Pancho saw that our friend Aguila was going to be drunker than he has ever been in his life, he sent Angel to follow. When Aguila gets so drunk he falls down for good, then Angel will bring up the carriage and we will load our drunk friend. The man is small, is he not?"

"About a pistol-barrel span," agreed Milton.

"And his woman, his wife, ah, such a beauty. She is of normal size. And all of their children are the same. Size does not count with women. It is not what a man has, it is how he uses it." Medero said, laughing. He looked back at the little man following slowly. "Sí, we will put our friend into the vehicle and little Angel will whisk him home."

"More like pour him into it," Milton said in one of his rare attempts at humor. He still didn't know who Angel was and why he had not seen him before.

Medero dropped back to tell the joke to his lieutenant friend. They were still laughing when they entered the busy cantina.

All of the tables were full as they walked into the main room, but one was quickly cleared for the four men. Of these four one was of the wealthy of San Antonio, two were military officers of the garrison, and one was of the breed of men you did not care to say no to. If you did, you said it very quietly, very politely, and with a smile.

The cantina was full of merrymakers. Soldiers and civilians mingled in a joyful gathering, for this day also fell on the day the soldiers had been paid. All were doing their best to spend a month's meager pay in one night. Then they would spend the rest of the month in the barracks or borrow money from some shylock at exorbitant rates.

When drinks were brought, Aguila downed his in one swallow. It seemed that the noise and music had given him new life and stiffened his rubbery legs. He got to his feet and, with a slight bow to his friends, weaved his way to grab a young girl as a dance partner. He and the girl took over the dance floor, much to everyone's delight. Aguila was one of those people who become more enjoyable and in love with the world when drunk. He immediately fell in love with every girl he saw. He loved everyone, and it was hard to become angry with him. Before he got the chance to become hard to handle, he would pass out as if he had suddenly been stunned by a blow on the head. Then he would sleep in blissful peace for ten straight hours.

A dark young man with curly black hair and a thin mustache pushed his way through the throng. "Hey, Monsieur Milton Hicks!" he called.

Milton shook the proffered hand of Jean du Bois. "How do?"

"Fine. Long time no see," Du Bois said. He shook hands with the two army officers.

Milton didn't know much about Jean du Bois. In fact, no one did. Like many who came to Texas—Mexican or Anglo—there was an untold story behind him. It was believed that he was the son of one of Napoleon's bodyguards who had been exiled from France and came to the United States in 1815 in search of a new home. Du Bois could have left the States for the same reason the Bowie brothers had left—feuding and dueling. The young Frenchman was of that temperament. Jean had arrived in de Bexar without a dime, speaking only French and poor English and looking as if he had not eaten in weeks. He had been taken in by an old man who owned a number of warehouses in San Antonio. There was no doubt that the young Frenchman was a man of quality and intelligence. Within weeks he was able to converse in Spanish and had become the most valuable man at the warehouses. He became

head bookkeeper and was becoming responsible for more and
more of the business.

"Sit down and join us, Jean," Medero told the Frenchman.

"Thank you. I will buy the next bottle of wine," Jean told
them in nearly flawless Spanish. In the past twelve years he
had become as much Mexican as any Mexican who had been
born here. He looked at Aguila dancing. "The wine will be for
everyone except our good friend who is making a fool of himself on the dance floor."

The men at the table laughed. It was not a laugh you used
when laughing at a fool but one of affection for a friend.

Aguila finished the dance and walked back to the table, arm
in arm with the girl. He strutted, puffed up with pride from
the loud approval of the crowd. The woman he had been crying to Milton about just minutes before was now forgotten.
Aguila sat down in his chair and pulled the girl into his lap.
All the men at the table knew the young woman and smiled at
her as the two sat down. She was a pretty little thing and they
all liked her. But none came to her rescue. It was her job to
keep Aguila occupied, and she was an expert at her job.

He tried to fondle her breast, but she easily pushed his
hands aside. It would have been just as easy to escape his grasp
if she wished. Aguila was liked by all and she would take his
company, drunk or sober, over that of many others.

"I would say hello to our friend the Eagle, but I do not think
he would know I was here, or care," Du Bois said with a grin
on his handsome face.

"That is a very accurate summation," Medero returned with
a grin.

"He has drunk enough to bring a mule to its knees," Ybarra
said in amazement. "I knew our old friend could outdrink any
of us at this table, but nothing like this!"

"I think this is one time el Aguila will not get by without a
dreadful hangover," Du Bois said, laughing.

To the amazement of all who knew Aguila, he could drink
all night and, after his ten hours' sleep, awake with neither

bloodshot eyes nor a heavy head. But they were sure he would not escape the common fate this time.

"I think he is more interested in *puta*," Ybarra said.

The girl felt between Aguila's legs and shook her head. "No!" she said with a giggle.

A group of Anglos jumped to their feet and one called a hill-country square dance. Strange as it seemed, the call blended with the Mexican tune. The mountain men from the United States jumped and stomped, sweat running into their heavy mulehide boots and making a squishing sound at every step. The dance of these strangers was crude, with little or no rhythm. Their stomping and yelling seemed coarse and out of place to these fun-loving Mexicans.

"Amigo, since the law of 1830 was passed, banning all Americans from coming into Mexico, it seems that more and more of that breed comes," Jean du Bois said to Milton. "I do not wish to anger you, mi amigo, but some of your fellow Yanquis are not such good men. I think maybe Mexico should try harder to enforce that law."

"You do not anger me, and these men are not my fellow Yanquis," Milton told him. "These men are considered trash by their own fellow mountain men. I have seen true mountain men, both French and American. These men would never make the grade."

"I think their fellows are right in not liking them," Medero put in. "These kinds of men have been nothing but trouble since they came to Mexico. They do not respect the customs of Mexico, they do not respect Mexican law, and I think maybe they do not even respect themselves."

Milton agreed with him. He had seen too many of these types of men before leaving his mountain home in U.S. territory. To their way of thinking anyone not of Anglo-Saxon origin or their type of Christianity was not much higher than an animal. Yet most of them were illiterate themselves. They treated their women as mere objects of pleasure, to be used to mother children and as draft animals. Now they were coming here.

A huge mountain of a man walked over to the table. His beard needed trimming, and it was stained with tobacco juice. His buckskins were dirty with grease and in need of repair. They stank as bad as they looked, and a stale, sour smell came from his person that could have been detected over the stench of an angered skunk. He roared from behind his tobacco-stained beard, "Let me have that lil' senorita! Let her dance with a real he-man and not some drunkin' dainty she-man of a Meskin!"

All of this was said in English, and only Milton and Jean understood it. Nonetheless, the Mexicans comprehended his tone of voice.

The mountain man grabbed the girl by her wrists to pull her from Aguila's lap. Aguila had passed the point where he could stand again, let alone defend himself against such a man.

Milton looked at the girl and saw disgust mixed with concern in her dark eyes. She strained against his hold on her, but he easily jerked her to her feet. Her arm was locked in an iron grip and he was as unmovable as a great oak tree.

Milton looked quickly at his friends and knew that they would fight before they would let these Americans run over them. They would protect their women, even if she was a cantina dancer and a prostitute. He also knew that his two friends and the two army officers were no match for these huge men from the mountains. If by some chance the Mexicans did win in a fight, it would not be before many of their men were killed and injured. Quick, decisive action had to be taken, and it had to be brutal enough to get these mountain men's attention. Milton smiled inwardly. This was turning out to be an exciting evening after all.

"Friend, you can take your hands off the girl," Milton said in excellent English.

The man gave him a surprised look. "Wal, wal! Looky here, boys! A Mex thet kin talk American! I didn't know they made 'em thet smart down here."

"You smart enough to speak Spanish?" Milton asked with a slight smile. There was no humor in his pale blue eyes.

"Wal, hell no! But I don't got to!" he roared.

His followers laughed. One put in, "I didn't knowed they made men thet tall down here in Mex country."

The cantina became quiet; the band had ceased to play. There was nothing new about an occasional fight in a cantina, but everyone knew this one could turn into a real bloodletting.

"Then I suggest you do two things, which you may find yourself having to do anyway. Turn that girl loose, and go back to the States where you belong and you don't have to speak Spanish." It was a long speech for Milton, and it was stated in the same even, unemotional tone he always used. No one could tell by his outward appearance that his nerves were wound tight and he was ready for action.

"An' jest who the goddamned hell says so?" the mountain man asked.

"Milton Hicks."

"Wal, now thet jest don't mean one goddamned thing to this lil' 'ole chile. An' I'm Ward Smiley, if'n thet means anythin' to you," Smiley said with sarcasm. "An' what's gonna happen if'n I don't let go?"

"It means I'm going to take out this big knife of mine, shave off that dirty beard so I can find your throat, then cut it from ear to ear," Milton told him.

Smiley roared with mock laughter.

Jean du Bois stood up, but he held his peace. Medero and Ybarra couldn't understand what was being said, but they could tell by the tone and attitude of the two men that it was leading up to a possible killing. Medero started to stand up and exert his authority, but he knew it would neither halt nor impress these two men.

"I ain't lettin' go of this here little Meskin gal," Smiley told Milton.

Everyone held his breath, afraid he might miss something.

"It just might cost you a hand."

"Like hell it will!"

Keeping his eyes on Smiley, Milton shrugged his broad shoulders and stood up. In one fluid motion he pulled out the long, heavy-bladed knife and with one powerful stroke cut the man's hand off at the wrist.

Smiley gave a surprised look, and as the pain registered in his whiskey-soaked brain, he gave out a loud bellow mixed with pain and anger. He suppressed his scream by clamping his lower lip between his teeth. Blood flew over his beard as he bit through his lower lip. With a roar that sounded more animal than human, he lunged at the man who had amputated his right hand.

Milton stood his ground. Shifting the knife into his left hand, he drew his pistol and hit the charging man alongside his head. The barrel smashed the top of his left ear, mangling it beyond repair. The blow stopped the huge man, but he did not fall. Milton gave Smiley a sharp rap on the back of the head, and he crumpled to the floor in a heap. Milton swung around to face the other Americans, his pistol at the ready.

Everyone in the room stood petrified, looking in amazement at the severed hand hanging on to the girl's arm. Medero reached over and pulled the hand from her wrist. The girl fainted.

The mountain men started pushing people to one side to make a clear path between them and Milton. Men and women obliged and quickly vacated the area. Eight of them faced Milton, two of whom he knew.

"Milton! Milton Hicks! I know you air a meaner man than airy one of us. But, can'tcha see, there air eight of us. Even you ain't thet big," one of the men said.

"You're running with bad company, Jake," Milton said.

"Yep, reckon I am. An', come hell and brimstone, I'll stick with 'em," said Jake, sure of himself.

"Jake, I only have one pistol and one knife, so I don't reckon I can get all of you. But I can guar-ran-tee you one goddamn thing that's a certain fact. You will be the first one to meet Satan in hell," Milton told him bluntly, aiming the pistol at Jake's chest.

"Ha, ha! Listen to thet breed bastard talk, would ya? He gets down here amongst these chili peppers an' he thinks he kin act an' talk jest like a white man. Back in Alabama we know how to handle you damned Injuns," O'Rourke told Milton.

Jean stepped forward and said in broken English, "He is not alone, monsieurs."

"Wal, wal! Would you looky here," one of the men roared with laughter. "A breed Injun an' a Frenchy gonna go up against real he-mountain men. Why, Frenchy, we air half alligator an' half mountain lion, an' all one hundert percent stud. We'll whop up yore wine-smelling breath an' never break into a sweat. We'll take out our big knives an' cut the lace clean off'n them silk drawers of yore'n."

"Monsieur, let me assure you that more then sweat will be shed if you persist in your show of animosity against my good friend Milton Hicks," Jean warned him.

"Lawdy, lawdy! Would you listen to thet Frenchy usin' them big American words. I wonder if he kin fight as good as he kin talk?" the man asked his friends.

Medero walked in between the men. The effects of the wine had left his face and he stood stiffly at military attention, facing the eight men with his authority. "*Alto!* There will be no further trouble. You men will take this injured one and depart immediately! Now!" he told them in Spanish.

"What'd he say, Jake? You understand them people's talk," one of the men said.

Jake told them, then turned back to Medero with a laugh. "Who said, Meskin?"

"I, Juan Yolanda Medero y Zaragosa, Capitán of the Mexican army. I will uphold my sworn duty to enforce the laws of my government. Now, I order you to disperse! Immediately! At once, or I will call the guard!"

Jake held a short conference with his friends.

"He can't do nothin'," one of the mountain men said. "He ain't no real law, jest a soldier boy an' we air civilians."

"That's wrong," Jake told him. "This here is Mexico. They don't have a regular mayor down here like they do back in America. He is called an alcalde, which means 'political chief.'

He's the stud in charge of everything in his district. Thet's including the army."

The men held another short conference, then faced Milton and Medero. "Okay, senors, you got the upper hand this time an' it's a standoff. But I gar-un-tee you one thing, Milton Hicks. You ain't gonna live to see many more sunsets. We'll see thet you go to the sunset you Cherokee calls the land of the Black Man. The land of dead souls, an' you air gonna be one."

Medero had a brief conference with Jean, who was acting as his interpreter. "Senors," the captain told them, "if this man is set upon and killed by a group of men and not given a fair chance to defend himself, I will come after all of you. And, gentlemen, this Meskin will be able to arrest all of you. Because this one will have enough soldiers with him to do his duty. And listen to this also. If any of you are here in violation of our new immigration law of 1830, you had better not be here tomorrow. Now! For the very last time, disperse at once!"

"Okay, gentlemen," Jake said as sarcastically as he could, "but I warn you, Milton Hicks. You had better not come over to where them white folks' settlements are on the Brazos an' the Trinity. You ain't no frontier ranger for Austin right now."

"Jake, I go where I wish. Now take that trash with you and get out of town," Milton told him with finality.

"Then you'd better sleep with one eye open, else there air gonna be one less breed in this here country," Jake said with all the malice he could muster. Then he looked at Medero. "An', capitán, I been in Texas before this new law came in this year. By yore own law, I kin stay as long as I want to."

"Si, senor, that is true. But who knows how much of that time you will spend in the *calabozo*. The legal status of the other men may be questionable," Medero told him. His voice was becoming lower and was strained from holding back his anger.

Two men came forward and picked up their fallen comrade. One reached down and picked up the hand to carry with them.

Another senorita fainted.

Aguila sat in his chair unable to move but taking in everything with a strange smile on his handsome face. He watched the Americans leave. Turning his head to look at Milton he said, "Mi amigo, Don Milton! You have *muchos huevos grandes*. Your *heuvos* are as large as the stud horse!"

Aguila laughed gleefully and used one hand to bang on the tabletop. "This calls for a drink! Everyone will drink! It will be paid for by me, I, Ricardo Alvino Ignacio Hernandez, el Aguila! We will honor our brave friend, Don Milton!"

Two men picked up the girl who had fainted in Aguila's lap and carried her away.

Aguila raised his glass and downed a large shot of the fiery tequila. This last drink was enough to finish him. His head suddenly dropped to the table as if he had been shot. Blood trickled from his nose as his face smashed against the hard tabletop. He had ended his night early and would go home to have a restless night dreaming of the beautiful Alicia. He would wake tomorrow with a swollen head and sore nose.

Milton, Jean, and the two army officers carried Aguila out to the waiting carriage. Angel saluted the four gentlemen and drove away with a broad smile. His patron would suffer for this night.

Milton bid his friends good night and went back to the Cantina del Toro Negro, and Velia. He knew that because of the mountain men he would have to sleep with extra care while on the trail, but he did so at all times anyway. He was sure he would be safe in San Antonio.

He was tired and ready for a good night's sleep. But Velia would keep him awake for a while tonight.

Chapter Eight

Milton woke with the dawn, feeling the effects of the wine and tequila only slightly. He lay on the floor, having escaped from the uncomfortable contraption the white man called a bed sometime during the night. His trade blanket was his mattress and his bedroll his pillow.

Two flies did acrobatics overhead as they tried to mate in midair. A collision caused them to give up and they flew out of an open window. Milton turned his head to see a long-legged spider cross the floor with its bouncy, unsteady walk.

He slipped into his moccasins and buckskin shirt, then stood up and looked down at the woman. She was partly covered by the bed sheet even though it was hot. Both breasts were bare as she lay on her back. He smiled at the joy he had received in kissing those breasts. That was the white man's blood in him. He was glad it came out in him at times. To the Cherokee the breasts were nothing but a source of food for the young. Before the white man's Christian missionaries came among the Cherokee, bare breasts were a common thing, especially in hot weather. Now the Cherokee had become "civilized" and Christianized. They were aware that such things as improper clothing could get you sent to the white man's hell!

He quietly walked across the room, tied his pistol, tomahawk, and knife around his waist, picked up his shot bag, powder horn and rifle, and eased out the door. When he got to the bottom of the stairs, Maria stood watching him with the same expression of desire in her soft brown eyes he had seen the day before. By this time next year she would find someone to satisfy those desires. He would do it himself, but he knew it would cause more trouble than it was worth.

"*Buenos dias*, Maria."

"*Buenos dias*, Don Milton," she returned. Her eyes dropped as if she was afraid they might reveal her inner thoughts.

If I didn't have more than I could handle upstairs I would give that young lady that satisfied look right now, he thought. Most Cherokee girls were married and with child at her age. Then he asked, "Is breakfast ready?"

"Sí. There is chili con carne, frijoles, and tortillas."

"Put in some fried eggs and plenty of coffee," he told her.

"There is plenty of coffee." She gave one last smile and went into the kitchen. She returned shortly with his breakfast. It was a huge breakfast for a huge, active man.

Milton even ate a few of the hot peppers. When he finished his breakfast, he went out back to the tack room and got his saddle. He planned to do some hunting before the heat of the day began.

He rode west out of town to the banks of Zarazamore Creek. The creek was beginning to dry up in the summer heat. He had not ridden far before he had flushed and killed two turkeys. A wild turkey is among the hardest wild game to hunt, and only the best marksman could have killed two with a long rifle.

Before he had ridden to the head of the drying creek he killed a large buck. This would keep Lupe's kitchen in meat for a couple of days. He did not forget to ask the animals' spirits to forgive him before he squeezed the trigger.

Milton dressed out the deer and threw the carcass across the back of his saddle. The little pony stood its ground. A war horse has no fear of the smell of blood.

The trail along the banks of the creek were closed from the rest of the world by large oak, pecan, and hackberry trees covered with Spanish moss and a thick growth of underbrush. There were also willows on the banks and in the middle of the creek bed.

Milton smelled a campfire and white men before he rode

into the open area. Squatting around an open campfire were Jake and three of his friends. The man who had lost his hand to Milton's knife lay asleep under a large moss-covered oak tree. An empty bottle lay at his side, more lay around him.

Milton stopped his horse and his eyes swept the camp in a rapid glance. They were the only men in camp. The other three must have found a couple of old broken-down whores who did not care who crawled into bed with them.

"Wal, wal, if'n it ain't the big Milton Hicks in person," Jake said, standing up. He didn't look any better in the full light of day than he did at night under artificial light. His beard was as dirty and as much in disarray as that of the man with the missing hand. His lips were too full and red, moist all the time. He had a prominent paunch and his heavy shoulders drooped. He was probably in Texas because better men had run him out of the mountains.

The other three men were nothing unusual, just as dirty as Jake in their grease-stained buckskins. None of them gave Milton any real worry and he ignored them contemptuously.

"Hey, Jake, thet's thet Meskin thet cut poor ole' Ward's hand off, ain't he?" one of the men asked.

"I keep tellin' ya he ain't no Mex. He kin jest talk their talk real good, thet's all," Jake told him.

"Wal, he's as black as them niggers in de Bexar, even if they do call themselves Meskins," the other commented.

"He ain't nothin' but a damned breed Injun," Jake said, turning to Milton. "Is them lace-shirted lil' Meskin boys as good in bed as their lil' gals, Mr. Hicks? They's sure sissyfied lookin' dudes, they are."

The men laughed loudly, slapping their thighs.

Milton did not laugh. The thought of such an unhuman thing made him shudder inside.

The tall breed looked steadily at Jake with hard eyes. "Jake, when that wounded man is ready to ride, which had better be this afternoon, you boys mount up and head on outta here."

"Hell, this man's nearly dead as it is," Jake growled. "He

woulda bled to death if'n we hadn't stuck a hot iron to his
stub. He ain't gonna be fit to ride thet soon."

"If I see any of you in Mexico after today I'll kill you on
sight," Milton informed them. His manner was so quiet and
easy that it was hard to take him seriously.

The men laughed loudly at first. But under the stare of this
man their hee-hawing quickly changed to nervous giggles.

Milton sat easily in his saddle above them, the stern, impassive look of an Indian god on his face. His weapons were not
the fire, lightning, and thunder of the gods but those of mortal
man. He held his rifle in the crook of his left arm. With his
pistol, tomahawk, and knife handy, he knew that he could kill
three and maybe all four men before they could get to their
rifles. From the look in their eyes the men, too, were beginning to believe he could.

Every man must have at least some bluster to show his fellow man that he is not all coward. Milton understood and
would allow for this.

"Yeah, Mr. Hicks, you jest mite not git outta this here camp
alive. What makes you think you air big enough ter ride off
from here, bein' there's four of usuns and you ain't got no
backin'?" Jake asked.

Milton had heard it all last night. He replied calmly, "If I
don't, neither will three of you, an' I haven't made up my
mind which three it will be."

"Now jest a goddamned minute?" Jake ejaculated. "What
gives you the right to run us outta Mexico? You got no legal
right atall! None atall!"

"True, no legal right. But maybe I got a moral right,"
Milton said, grinning.

"Moral!" one of the men bellowed.

"Yeah. Mexico don't need none of you," Milton told him.
"My knife an' tomahawk thirst for your blood. That's another
right. Remain in Texas, and they will drink their fill."

Without another word he rode through their camp, turning
his back on them in a show of contempt.

The four men stood looking from one to the other, undecided as to what course of action they should take. Two jumped aside as Milton rode by. His little war pony must have felt their hostility because it bared its teeth as it walked past the men.

One of the men eased over to stand next to the tree where his rifle leaned. He stood unmoving, not sure of his ability to kill this man even by shooting him in the back. Maybe Hicks was as good as Jake said. He knew if he missed or didn't wound mortally with the first shot it just might be his last. This tall man was unsettling. He walked back to his friends without his rifle. "Hell! We can't do nothin' to this stinkin' breed bastard," he said. "If'n we do, we'll have thet Meskin cap'n down on us fer shore."

This was a way out.

"Ain't thet a fact. We can't do airy thing. Nothin'!" Jake agreed.

"It's a goddamned good thing for thet Mr. Milton Hicks!"

"Yeah! We woulda sculpped thet nigger for shore!"

The four stood a few minutes discussing what they would have done to Milton Hicks had they had the chance. They finally got down to the question of where they were going from here. One suggested a town called Taos, west of there. It was outside Texas and too far for the Mexican captain to get word to the authorities there even if he wanted to. American and French fur trappers went to Taos to sell their furs and rendezvous. He included himself and the others among the fur trappers and western mountain men's breed by stating that they were mountain men "jest lak us'n."

It was agreed that that was where they would go, just as soon as the other men came back to camp. Smiley would be able to ride by this afternoon. If he made the trip, fine. If not, who would mourn his passing? Even his poor old mother wasn't around to grieve the loss. Smiley and his two brothers had killed her in one of their drunken brawls years before.

The men broke camp and waited for the other three to return. If they didn't make it back soon, they were going to have to look out for themselves.

The men thought their ride to Taos would be no more than the ride from the eastern part of the United States to Texas had been. They could not have anticipated the three ominous things waiting for them on a trip across West Texas. Those three things were the Llano Estacado, the Comanche, and the Kiowa.

Milton rode back to the village. One woman was waiting for the fresh meat he was carrying; another was waiting for him to make her happy.

Chapter Nine

Milton swung his feet over the side of the bed and sat up. He filled his clay pipe full of tobacco and fired it up. He seldom smoked. The best time was after a meal or something more satisfying. What he had just had was satisfying, and that was a fact.

Velia lay back in the bed, spent, her face and hair wet with perspiration. A small bead of sweat ran under her right breast and down her side. She smiled at the broad back of her lover. This man was much of a man. A tall, beautiful specimen of the male sex. He was *mucho hombre!* He was as big and strong as he looked. All the girls in de Bexar were jealous of her. And there were younger women than she who would try to steal him from her. And now there was also her sweet little adopted sister, Maria, who looked upon him with hunger and desire. She would have to watch that little one. Maria was in her time, and was as hot and bothered as a bitch in heat. Velia had seen Maria eyeing Milton ever since he had pulled off his shirt in the bathhouse. She had looked upon his huge, bare chest and had seen a man. *Mucho hombre!* But let some other man, not Milton, take her maidenhead and ease the passion in her heart, the lust in her eyes, and the ache between her legs.

She raised up on one elbow and kissed Milton on the back. "My big, big *mucho hombre grande,* why don't you stay here in San Antonia with me? We don't have to marry. I tell the priest he can go to hell!"

Milton smiled, but he kept his peace. Nothing needed to be said. She knew how he was and always would be. There was forever something, somewhere that he must find. A fight he must fight, rivers he must cross, mountains whose other side he must see. To be bound to a town or a white woman was to be bound by the foot. And to be bound by the foot meant a man must remain in one place and take root. If a man took root, he would ripen quickly, then rot for a long time and die badly. It would be the end of him, and he knew it, if he could never follow another sunset or see where the sunrise would find him. A man such as he who followed the sun might not live as many years as the man who took root and died slowly, and a free spirit may be short-lived. But, ah, in his short span on earth he would do three times the living as the man with roots.

"Well, I thought I would ask again," Velia said, breaking in on his thoughts. "I do every time, you know?"

He stood and pulled up his pants. The midday sun cast a hot glow through the open window.

There was a mad scramble up the stairs. The footsteps stopped outside the door.

"Don Milton! Don Milton, mi amigo! I must have your assistance, for the love of the Mother of God!" cried Aguila as he pounded on the door.

For Aguila to be this upset it must be something serious, Milton thought.

Velia covered herself with the sheet and Milton swung the door open. "What's wrong, my friend?"

"Pardón, senorita," Aguila begged of Velia. Milton liked him better for that. She was only a cantina singer and a prostitute, but Aguila did pause long enough to show that he was at least aware of her presence. "There is much trouble, amigo! Much trouble!"

"What kind?"

"Comanche!"

No doubt about it, that was trouble all right.

"Go downstairs and wait. I will be down." Milton closed the door and finished dressing. The noon heat was starting to make him feel as if the four walls of the room were closing in on him. He would be glad to get out in the open, even to follow Comanche.

"Velia, get my buckskins ready and pack some food and extra water. I'm sure we will have a long, hard ride if we chase Comanche," he told her. "And tell Jesús to saddle my horse and bring him around front with all my gear. He must have my rifle ready."

"You just get here and they take you away from me. I hate all of them," she said, pouting.

"You just rest up for when I return," he told her.

"Oh, that I will do, big man, that I will do. You will be dragging by the time I get through with you," she told him happily.

He was actually chuckling as he walked out the door.

Miguel was standing at the foot of the stairs when Milton came down. "It must be bad if Aguila acts like this. We cannot understand what he is talking about."

Milton and Miguel walked over to where Aguila was hopping from one foot to the other. He quickly stumbled over what had happened.

The home of Alicia's parents in the brush country had been raided by Indians the day before. Most of the vaqueros were with her father and two brothers taking cattle south to sell and only a few men had been left behind. The Indians held siege all night. Before dawn, José Sanchez, one of the vaqueros of the ranch, was able to slip away and come for help. José had run on foot for hours before he found a small estancia and commandeered their plow horse to ride the rest of the way. A group of men were now gathered in front of the alcalde's house.

Milton didn't say a word, but walked out of the cantina, followed by Aguila, Miguel, and the other men. As they neared the group in front of the old royal governor's house where the vice-governor now lived, Alicia saw them and broke away to meet them. A look of terror twisted her beautiful face.

"Oh, thank God you came!" she told Milton. Then she

turned to Aguila and made his day. "Oh, thank you, my friend! Thank you!"

When they walked up to the group of men and women, Milton could see the look of excitement and confusion on their faces. Everyone wanted to talk at once, and all of them had become instant experts on Indian fighting. Milton knew that this was one of those times when he must stand to one side and say nothing. It is impossible to talk sense to a senseless crowd.

"Todo el mundo, enviar los caballos de ustedes! Everyone, to your horses!"

"Apresurarse, muchachos! Hurry, boys!"

"Get your guns! Hurry! Let's go!"

"We meet on the edge of town!"

"On the road to Laredo!"

The men milled around the alcalde of San Antonio de Bexar, Ramón Musquiz. By his side stood Colonel Ruiz and Captain Medero. None of the three were able to quiet the people and get some semblance of order. The vice-governor, Juan Beramendi, stood on the porch of the governor's palace. This was a local matter and he would not interfere, but he would be ready to give any assistance the state or federal government could offer. Which was, in truth, very little. Colonel Ruiz and his few troops were all there was.

Milton pulled Aguila close to him and told him that they must not rush off half-cocked and unprepared. They may in all probability have to follow the Indians, and no one knew where that might lead. If they were indeed Comanche, they would have to go into the Llano Estacado of West Texas. Be prepared.

Aguila yelled loudly. When his voice began to get sore, he pulled his pistol and fired into the air. Everyone stopped talking and turned to him. "My pardons, Don Juan and Don Ramón, for firing the gun. Please, please, listen! All of you! My friend Don Milton, he has given me good counsel and he says that we must not rush off unprepared. We may have to follow the savages for many days. If they are Comanche, we will have to go into the Llano Estacado."

"Boo!" someone shouted from the back of the crowd. "We go, now! Our friends need our help!"

"Please, my friends! Please go prepared! The Indians have gone by now. We must take food and water and ammunition!"

"We will get it at the ranch!"

"There may be none left when we get there!" Aguila told them.

"We do not need counsel from that Anglo Yanqui! He does not need to tell us how to fight Indians!"

"Most of us Mexicans are part Indian ourselves," someone said, laughing.

"I am half. My mother is a Waco," another called out.

All the men laughed.

"Yes! We meet at the edge of town!"

"Juan Pérez can lead us!"

"And Tomás Gutierrez!"

"We meet at the edge of town!"

Most of the men ran from the assembled meeting. They ran in every direction at once, none seeming sure which way he should go. It would be the inexperienced leading the inexperienced. A number of children and village dogs ran through the street, adding to the confusion.

"Half Indian! Hump!" Miguel grunted. "He is a town Indian like the rest of us. A white man's town at that."

Colonel Ruiz walked over to Alicia and took both of her hands in his. "Senorita, it seems the army must stand to one side once more and watch civilians take care of the problems of the frontier. I have three patrols out at present and I must keep at least one fourth of my command in at all times. Those are the regulations. Your father, Don Raul, is an old and dear friend. You know that I would go to the aid of his family if it were possible."

"Yes, I know," Alicia said.

This is why I would not stay in an army. I go when and where I desire, Milton thought. The colonel's hamstrung by orders and regulations.

"Don Milton is correct. The men should not rush off unprepared. He gives good counsel," the colonel told the remaining men.

"I must get ready," Alicia told them. "I will go with the first group of men. I must get to my mother."

Aguila looked quickly at Milton. Milton nodded his head.

"All right, senorita, we will go with this first group of men. I will be your escort and protector," Aguila informed her.

She gave him a grateful look. He was finally getting hold of himself and behaving in the manner of the responsible leader of men he always was. Henceforth he would no longer be the happy-go-lucky bachelor, buying wine for everyone and chasing every available girl. He would become a responsible man of business and take his place as a community leader.

Milton looked at his young friend and smiled inwardly. The breaking of the young man to the saddle had begun.

"You must ride a horse. A carriage will not keep up with the men," Aguila told her.

"Senor, I am a ranch girl. I can ride a horse like the wind," Alicia informed him, smiling. "That was before I went to the young lady's school in Mexico City."

The two laughed at their own personal joke.

Alicia turned to her aunt. "Tia, you stay here and come later in the carriage."

"No! My sister and her family are in danger. I will ride with you," Luz told her niece. "I was riding a horse long before you were even born, little girl."

Luz turned to the men. "Good day, gentlemen."

Pancho called to Aguila, "I will get all the supplies we need and bring them with me!"

"*Bueno!*"

A short time later the thunder of horses' hooves filled the air as the rescue party rode out.

Milton and Miguel walked back to the cantina. Miguel spoke. "Do you think the Comanche will still be around when they arrive at the ranch?"

"No," Milton told him in a matter-of-fact voice. "Whether they be Comanche, Lipan, or Mescalero, they will be gone by the time they get there. It will be a raiding party, looking for horses. They know that many ranch men are gone, and they could come back at any moment. If they have captives, we will have to follow."

He paused, then said with a serious note in his voice, "I just hope they are not Comanche, or their cousins, the Kiowa."

"Aaaahhhhh! That is so. I would go, Don Milton, if I were at least fifty pounds less of soft fat." Miguel sighed. "And maybe a few years younger."

When they got to the front of the cantina Milton kissed Velia, to everyone's delight, patted Lupe on her shoulder, and shook hands with Miguel. Maria eased forward and gave Milton a kiss. It was supposed to be a shy one from one who was so young, but it was wet and sensuous. Velia pulled Maria away from him.

Milton swung into the saddle and took his rifle and shot pouch from Jesús. Then he slung two water canteens across the pommel. He had plenty of powder and shot, and his percussion caps were the best, made of fulminate of mercury in copper caps and not of the paper type that was more subject to the elements. A hunter of animals could afford a misfire. A hunter of men could not. Without a backward glance, he rode off.

"Come back to me, you big donkey," Velia said softly.

Lupe put her heavy arms around Velia and held her close.

Pancho was the first to join Milton on the road south of town. Milton reminded him that if the Indians had taken captives from the ranch, this could be a long, hard ride.

Pancho informed Milton, a large grin on his heavy face, that he would still be in the saddle long after the young, skinny ones had fallen out.

Milton just bet he would be one of the last to quit. This was one man they would not have to worry about on this trip.

Chapter Ten

Smoke from a dying fire could be seen rising slowly in the windless sky above the chaparral. Pancho spurred his big Andalusian war horse to a faster pace. The big horse was the strain the Spaniards had bred for use during the days of armor. No other horse but the big steel-gray could have carried the heavy man these forty miles in such a short time. The big Mexican pointed to the column of smoke.

Milton was already aware of the smoke, having seen signs of it in the sky thirty minutes before. It was not true that an Indian had the eyes of an eagle, however. The red man was trained as a boy to not only see things but be able to distinguish one thing from another. Milton knew there was a possibility that some of the ranch buildings would still be burning when they arrived, therefore he was looking for smoke.

The group of armed men rode into the front yard of the main ranch house just before sunset. The house had been set afire, but the fire had been contained in one small wing of the adobe building. The barn, with some winter hay left inside, was the source of the smoke the arriving men had seen. Only a smoldering heap was left.

Aguila walked out to meet the men. He did not go to Juan Pérez, the Mexican leader of this second group, but directly to Milton. "It is bad, amigo. Very bad."

"It usually is when Comanche are involved," was Milton's only comment.

Juan Pérez and Pancho joined them. A worker of the ranch came and led their tired horses away to be watered and fed.

The men's mounts were so tired that even Milton's little Indian pony did not object to a stranger handling it.

"What has happened, my son?" Pancho asked, expecting the worst.

"Bad things! Bad! The Indians—they were Comanche— killed Pedro, Alicia's younger brother, the priest from the mission, and four vaqueros. A woman of the house was killed and three injured. Alicia's mother, the Dona Ysabela, was not injured, nor was Alicia's sister, Olivia," Aguila told them quickly. "The worst part is, they have captured a little fourteen-year-old sister of Alicia's, Josephine. She had been out riding when they attacked. She was caught before she could ride to safety."

"Are you sure they were Comanche?" asked Juan.

"For sure. They were seen and enough sign is here," Aguila told him.

"Which direction did they take?" Milton asked.

"South. They also came from that direction," said Aguila.

José Sanchez, the vaquero who had ridden to San Antonio for help, came forward. "Senors, I request politely for permission to speak."

"Of course, José, you have it," Aguila told the vaquero. Everyone noticed that Aguila had taken charge now that they were at the ranch.

He was submitting to the bridle and the bit. Next would come the saddle and spurs. Milton smiled.

"My friend Polo Lopez, he say he has a body of one Indian. He say he be Comanche. Kwaharie Comanche!" José informed the men. "Please, come with me."

"Kwaharie! Bah! That band roams far out on the Llano Estacado. They don't attack this far south and east. And if they did, it would be from the north or northwest," Juan Pérez snorted. There were many Mexicans of full-blood Spanish descent who held little or no respect for the peons of mixed Indian and Spanish blood. Juan was among those who openly showed his feelings. "They were probably not even Comanche. Maybe Lipan or Mescalero Apache. They raid this far east and south, and all the way to the coast."

"I am humble and beg your pardon, sir. My friend Polo, his mother's mother is Comanche and Kiowa. She is of the Comanche band, the Penateka, the Honeyeaters," José told him politely.

Milton motioned for José to lead the way. Talk would not settle the dispute, only evidence.

As they walked, Aguila told Milton and Juan, "Some of the men in the first group went south to follow the Indians' trail. Many of the men who are still here wish to go back to de Bexar."

"Huh," Milton grunted without further comment.

"Some of the men do not wish to fight," Juan said with disgust.

The men followed José to the front of the gutted barn and horse stalls. An Indian lay stretched out on the ground and two Mexican vaqueros stood near him. The Indian had posted himself too far from his friends for them to reach him when the battle was over. From his dress and markings he was indeed a Comanche, the band that called themselves Kwaharie, "Antelope." The high plains of West Texas, the area the Spanish had named the Llano Estacado, or "Staked Plains," was sectioned off by the Comanche for use by separate bands of the tribe. The Kwaharie roamed the southern part of the Llano, but the Comanche bands wandered freely in each other's territory. There were four large bands and some smaller ones, making up the loose-knit Comanche confederacy. The braves were so wild, unruly, and individualistic that no single chief had ever been strong enough to bring all the bands together to form one large tribe.

"Antelope, not Honeyeaters," Milton said bluntly. "And they're sure not Apache."

Polo Lopez, who was standing next to the dead Indian with Eduardo Gutierrez, nodded his head in agreement.

Juan sputtered but said nothing. He was being upstaged by a peon with the aid of a Yanqui.

"Blessed Holy Mother of Jesus!" exclaimed Pancho, crossing himself. "The Kwaharie! We should pray for ourselves before we go after them."

To chase the Kwaharie meant they were not only after some of the best warriors on horseback in the world, but they also had to face the Llano Estacado. Between the two evils the entire party would probably be lost. Many parties of white men had entered the Llano Estacado never to be heard from again. Only those who had never seen the huge, flat, dry plains would be unable to appreciate these men's fear of them. The water holes were known only by the Indians that roamed the plains, and the Llano Estacado was so flat and free of any distinguishing marks that it was easy for a man to lose his way. For that reason the first Spaniards to cross the plains without an Indian guide placed stakes from line of sight to line of sight to guide them back across on their return to Mexico.

Yes, we may lose all of our men, thought Pancho. But is that not the way when men go off to make war?

"This man is a *pukutsi*," Milton told the men.

The *pukutsi* was out in front of his raiding friends because a *pukutsi* is an overly reckless brave who is afraid of nothing. He does not fear death itself. The *pukutsi* was considered crazy by his own people, yet at the same time they couldn't help but admire and respect him. He did everything backward. He bathed in mud, then dried in water. He would ride his horse backward, giving commands for left when he meant right and right when he meant left. Since he was on the horse backward, his commands would come out properly and his horse was never confused. The *pukutsi* had rather be killed in battle than show cowardice. He carried a sash over his shoulder and rolled up under his arm. When the fighting started, he unrolled his sash, stuck the free end into the ground with an arrow or lance, and there he took his stand. With his buffalo scrotum rattle in one hand and bow in the other, he stood singing his war songs until victory was won or death took him. Only a friend could free him. Should he give way in battle or release himself after the fight was done, the other warriors would taunt him into an overt act against them so they could kill him. The warrior in front of them was still tethered by his sash.

"Do you think we should follow the Comanche into the Llano Estacado?" Juan asked. This was not a coward asking the question in fear but a practical man asking a practical question.

"We go now, as soon as the horses are watered and fed," Milton told him. There was no question as to what he would do. A fight was food for the soul of a warrior, and this was going to be a fight.

"Now? We go right now and it is getting dark? Man, are you crazy?" asked Juan.

A strained look came over his face for being so foolish with this tall Yanqui, but he stood his ground as only a man of quality could do.

Milton took no notice of him. There were more important things at hand.

The men looked at Milton with blank stares. One did not track Indians at night—not even other Indians.

"We head north by northwest," Milton suggested. "The Penateka Comanche are in the south. Since there have been no changes in the assigned territory of the Comanche, the Kwaharie are located to the north of them in the Llano Estacado. That is to the northeast of us."

"Now he gives a lesson in geography," Juan said, butting in.

Milton looked at Juan a moment. I let you by once, but don't make a habit of it, he said to himself. Then he continued: "I know the route the Kwaharie take when they cross the plains, and their favorite routes to and from them. They have left here by going south, to fool the white man. They will go south for a while. Then they will camp for the night. Tomorrow, before the other search party catches up with them, they will eat their fill of mule meat and then go home to the Llano Estacado. This was a raiding party, not a war party. They have their horses and a captive, so they will not linger in white man's land."

"The poor girl," Juan said. "Among those savages."

Polo wished to speak in defense of the Indians, but he was only a breed vaquero of the hacienda. He held his tongue.

Milton was a breed Indian, but he was not a peon to hold his tongue when he wished to speak. "Yes, she will be raped," he told them. "The Comanche have no more respect for Mexican women than you have for Comanche women, whom you rape with impunity. She will not be murdered. They may use her as trade or as a wife."

"All right. We will go now. It is settled," Aguila said with a voice of command.

Juan looked sharply at Aguila in the failing light. "So now you have voted yourself the leader?"

"I will be in command. Dona Ysabela will wish it. We, the ranch people and my people, will provide the best men for tracking the Comanche," Aguila told him.

"We will provide the best men for tracking," mocked Juan. He wiped the sweat from his face with a huge neckerchief.

"Sí. The vaqueros and my men are wise in the ways of the trail. Can you say as much, amigo?" Aguila asked with raised eyebrows.

Milton smiled to himself, and Pancho smiled openly.

Jean du Bois came in from searching the area for stray horses. He and his men had found none.

Milton rode out to check the trail of the Indians. It was crisscrossed in many places by the pursuing white men, but he determined that there were fifteen ponies that were being ridden and one pony carrying double. Sixteen warriors and the girl. There were also seventeen other horses and nine mules being driven by the warriors. These were the animals stolen from the ranch. Soon there would be one less mule, Plains Indians preferring mule meat over all other except buffalo. He rode back to the main house as the men were getting ready to leave.

"One more question, if you please?" Juan asked Aguila.

"Proceed, Don Juan," Aguila told him.

"Why, I pray to the Blessed Son of God, do we leave now

when it is dark and on tired horses, ridden by equally tired men?" Juan asked, throwing his hands into the air and casting his eyes skyward. He was ever the dramatist.

Aguila looked at Milton, wanting him to speak and give an answer all of them could live with.

"Because, senor, I have studied the Comanche for many years and I think I know them well. I know some of the evasion routes of the Kwaharie. And I know how they travel," Milton told him quietly. "The raiding party will not go far today. They will travel just far enough to outdistance a rescue party. Then they will stop, kill a mule, and eat their fill. Tomorrow they will turn to the north. They will travel along the edge of the Llano, and then they will go into it at a point I know.

"We will go north from here, keeping to the west of de Bexar, keeping to the wood line and to the mountains. We will intercept them west of the old abandoned Real Presidio de San Saba. That is, if we leave tonight."

Juan shrugged his shoulders. There was no question about this man's courage and bravery. But there is someone like Juan Pérez in every group. There would be an argument every step of the way with him along. Aguila wished he had stayed at home in San Antonio.

Milton was different. He would have no trouble with Juan. If he didn't like a man, he simply stayed out of the man's way and did not associate with him any more than was necessary. If things got out of hand while in the company of these Mexicans, he would simply saddle his pony and ride off after the Comanche alone. He had made up his mind that he would bring back the girl. The pact he made with himself could be broken only by death.

Jean du Bois rode up alongside Milton and spoke for the first time. The Frenchman was as tired as the others, but there was a light, happy grin on his face. "My friend, I am one who will go where you say. I will leave the commanding and arguing to others."

"That makes two of us," Pancho added.

Milton smiled in the dim light of the setting sun. The sun was a bright orange and cast its bright rays of light over the chaparral. It was a good day for dying. The sun shone all the way to the home of Black Man in the west, whose domain is death. Black Man would be the one to guide a Cherokee warrior to the home of Uguwiheyi, the Great Chief, the Supreme Ruler of the Universe. The thought came often to a warrior, and he took comfort in knowing that he was going to an afterlife.

Dona Ysabela came out of the house with the other women. She looked at the men. There was grief on her face. The strain of having a son killed in the raid and a daughter carried off by the Indians had deepened the lines in her face. But she stood straight and composed, as befitted a woman of her station. "Senors, I will put my daughter's life in the hands of you brave men and my trust in God. May the Blessed Mother go with you, and may you bring my little girl back home. Go with God."

The lady of the hacienda stood with her head held high and proud. This woman would cry but it would be later, in the privacy of her room. Some of the other women sobbed openly.

Alicia walked close to Aguila's horse and stood at the stirrup. Her face shone in the light of the torches. It bore a strained look, but like her mother, she did not cry openly before the world. "Aguila, please bring my sister home," was her only plea. She looked at Milton, but said nothing. That same plea was in her eyes, plus a plea for him to look after Aguila.

It looked as if the footloose and fancy-free Aguila was about ready for the saddle and spurs.

"I will bring back little Josephine or I will not come back alive," Aguila boasted.

Some of the men smiled openly, but neither Aguila nor Alicia saw them. The pride of his manhood made Aguila oblivious of everyone's presence. Alicia was proud to have a gentleman offer his life for her benefit.

Aguila wheeled his tired horse and led the men out of the yard. There were twenty-two men in number. Milton was glad that the number was small. They would travel faster and be more organized.

Some of the men were riding out on an adventure they would remember and talk about for the rest of their lives.

Chapter Eleven

Milton led the men north by northwest, skirting along the eastern edge of the high plateau region. The trail he made was through thick underbrush, the limbs of thorns leaving many cuts and scratches on the men's exposed skin. They were unable to see the deadly limbs in the dark and were at their mercy. The going got worse when, around midnight, they reached the hill country west of San Antonio. Thick cedar growths impaired their progress so much that Milton finally called a halt. The tired men climbed down from exhausted horses, unsaddled them, and made a cold camp.

Before the sun had begun to show its face to the world, the tall man prodded the men out of their blankets. They were to find that Milton was a hard, relentless, driving man who had physical strength and stamina beyond belief. Only the strong of heart, with physical stamina to match, would continue on this trip.

Milton asked the Comanche breed Polo Lopez to be his assistant in scouting. The Mexican vaquero grinned broadly at the request. With this vote of confidence, Milton had won over a man who would ride into the fires of hell at his command.

Juan looked at the vaquero and said to anyone who would listen, "Why would a man fight against his own kind?"

Milton looked up. Juan Pérez was getting on his nerves. "What do you mean, senor?"

"Well, the Indians are his mother's people. And they are his people, by rights, since it comes from his mother's side," Juan said. "In fact, he is brother to all the red devils in this land of ours."

"Red should not fight against red, huh?" Milton was not in the habit of baiting people.

"No, they should not. It is plain barbarism for a man to fight against his own race," Juan said smugly.

"Then I reckon it would be safe to say that England, Spain, France, and the rest of Christendom have been living for centuries in a state of barbarism," Milton told him.

With a disgusted growl, Juan went to saddle his horse.

"My friend, you do not say much to men you do not like, but when you do, wow! You can cut hell out of him," Jean said in English.

The rest of the day was spent struggling through the thick cedar stands and up and down rock slopes. Milton and Polo skirted as many of the hills as possible and still did their best to remain on a north by northwest course. Often they found it was faster to go around a particular mountain than straight over it.

It was a frustrating fourteen hours, and tempers began to fray. Juan Pérez was a man to question every act, but once a course of action was agreed upon, he stuck with it like a bulldog to the nose of an angry bull. Juan wore perfumed toilet water and lace-trimmed shirts, and could gossip with the upper crust of Mexican society. But there all effeminacy ended. When he was among men of the frontier he took on the stance and attitude of his conquistador ancestors who had marched over this new land before him. He brooked no faint of heart around him.

Before the halt that evening, two men made their apologies and started back to San Antonio. Aguila looked disappointed, Pancho looked disgusted, and Juan cursed openly. Milton was glad to see the men leave and hoped that others among the less zealous would depart before they entered the Llano Estacado. They were only fifty or so miles northwest of San Antonio. Now was the time for those who were weak of heart to leave.

Another man left the group to catch up with the two who had departed. Juan gave the man a withering cursing and told him that he hoped he ran into a band of Comanche. No man should ever wish the Comanche upon another man, be he red or white. A Comanche regarded most red men of another tribe as he would a white man—as an enemy. Only the Kiowa were friends of the Comanche.

"May *el diablo* be your brother," Juan angrily yelled at the back of the retreating man.

Milton smiled at the curse. Only in English could a man use four-letter, descriptive adjectives in a real curse. He had known some ten-year-old white boys back in the States who could put any Mexican to shame when it came to real cursing.

By the end of the third day the men had traveled 150 miles. They had been long miles, tearing the guts out of man and animal alike. Only the little Indian ponies of Milton and Polo, and Pancho's big gray seemed fit to continue.

They rode through the pass of Puerto de Baluartes, "Haven of the Strong," and camped at the remains of the old fort, the Real Presidio de San Saba. The old Spanish settlement had been abandoned sixty-two years earlier because of the Comanche. It was a testament the Comanche had given to the white man. They wished no one to enter their homeland, be they red or white, for they had killed the mission Indians as eagerly as the whites.

Milton pulled the saddle from his horse and rubbed the animal down. "I'm sorry, little brother, to treat you so ill. But we must go to the aid of a little sister who is in danger. I'm sure you understand."

Only Polo heard the tall man speaking to his horse. Milton was using a language that was beyond Polo's comprehension. He could not understand the words, but he knew their meaning. The big man rose another notch in the eyes of the simple vaquero. Any man who took good care of and talked to his horse must indeed be a man of honor. A man with much feeling and soul. Honor is very important to a Mexican.

After the small fires had been put out, Milton walked to the remains of the old mission. It had been gutted and the roof had fallen in many years ago. Only the thick adobe walls now stood, and the rains and wind were slowly washing and blow-ing them back into the earth. He stood a short while looking at this symbol of the white man's civilization sitting in the heart of the red man's civilization. Only fools or brave men would try to establish a village of their own in such a remote place. These white men of his white grandfather's people were both brave and foolish. A man had to be both for such a small number to try and establish a civilization of their own in such a hostile place.

Some said white men would never settle the land of the Comanche. Even if the Comanche and his cousin, the Kiowa, were run off, this land was too barren for use. But Milton did not think the white man would leave this land alone. The white man would find a way. If the white man could not find use for this land, he would be happy, for at least he would control it. To the white man control meant almost as much as use and ownership. If a white man could not control something, he would rather see it destroyed than used by the red man.

Milton returned to camp and lay on the hard ground fully clothed. His saddle was his pillow and the sky both his blanket and roof. He was more comfortable than the rest of the men. He was now in his natural element.

He was awake before dawn. He walked to where Aguila lay and gently shook him awake. Milton told the Mexican that he was going to scout ahead. Aguila was to let the men rest for two hours after the sun rose. Polo would lead them.

Milton saddled his horse and rode out of the camp. The little pony walked as quietly as his master, and no one was awakened. Polo would lead the party of men and meet him at noon. He hoped the men would listen to Polo and take all precautions. These Comanche warriors seemed able to smell out white men miles before they saw them. Knowing how often white men took a bath, he could understand why.

A few miles from camp he came upon the tracks of eight shod horses. They were more than a day old. A twisted smile played across his lips. It must be the eight fools from the mountains, he thought. Men from the east riding alone into

the Llano Estacado. They were indeed fools, and completely
unaware of their stupidity.

Within thirty minutes Milton saw buzzards circling overhead in the distance. When he came to a slight rise where the
buzzards were circling directly overhead, he got off his horse
and eased over the crest to have a look. Below in a small valley
a half dozen men lay staked out spread-eagle fashion. It was
obvious that all were dead. The men had been scalped and the
buzzards had already been at work. Milton could tell that they
were white men, Anglo at that. The Plains Indians of West
Texas did not bother most Anglo white men traveling in this
area if they were just riding through. But they may have believed these men were responsible for some atrocity. He had
heard that some Anglos had come upon a small camp of Kiowa, containing mostly children and women, and that all of
them had been slaughtered.

He got back on his horse and spurred it forward, riding
down into the shallow valley. Buzzards flew a short distance
or hopped to one side at the disturbance of this unwelcome
intruder. Milton noticed that the one-handed Ward Smiley
was among the dead. His old friend Jake and one other were
not among them. This group had not even made it to the
Llano Estacado.

From the sign, the group had been attacked by the Kiowa,
the only Indian tribe allowed to roam freely in Comanche
territory. The arrows used by the Kiowa had been left behind.
Neither the Kiowa nor the Comanche would reuse an arrow
that had killed for fear that the blood may lead the dead man's
or animal's spirit back to them.

If the two missing men were taken alive to the main camp of
the Kiowa for women and children's sport, they would wish a
million times that they had died with their friends. Contrary
to popular opinion, Plains Indians seldom tortured their captives. But they were experts when they decided to do it.

Milton rode through the carnage left by these nomads of the
Plains. The buzzards flew and hopped back to their meal,
fighting for a better seat at this table of violence. Shortly be-

fore noon he spotted sixteen riders. One of the Comanche raiders was absent. Had he been killed in a run-in with an enemy, or was he out scouting? Milton knew without really asking himself that the man was scouting ahead even though they were now in Comanche country. Only the wary lived long in this hard land. The main party of the raiding band rode as if they hadn't a worry in the world and there wasn't a white man within a thousand miles.

From his vantage point on top of a small rise Milton watched them. He saw a mounted man trot his horse up to the main body. Now their scout was accounted for. The scout had come from the south. The scout pointed to the south, and from his vantage point Milton could see the search party heading directly toward the Comanche raiders.

All of the search party was accounted for, excluding the three men who had left the day before. Polo was doing a good job of scouting. The breed vaquero was using the terrain effectively to keep himself hidden as much as possible. The rest of the men rode boldly in the open. The white man takes this land by numbers and mechanical means, not by intelligence, Milton thought with disgust.

If the Comanche had not known before that they were being followed, they knew it now. He hoped that the Indians would try to set up an ambush on the search party and leave the girl and horses with one or two guards. He knew that with his superior weapons he could handle two men easily. But there was no such luck. The Indians continued to move north.

Now that the Comanche knew they were being followed, all hope for surprise was gone. He cursed the white men and his friend Aguila. The men had not waited for him but had gotten into their saddles and ridden hell-bent-for-leather after him. Now they were known to be in the private domain of the Comanche, the edge of the Llano Estacado, and they would pay for their carelessness with their lives. Soon the Comanche would head northwest and enter the rolling sea of grass. Then they would go to their main camp, which could be in any direction. And on the flat Llano there would be no folds of land or stands of timber for the white men or the red men to hide their movements. Each party would be able to see the other's every movement for miles in all directions in the open plains. And the Comanche had the advantage. Not only were they now operating in their own homeland, they also had exchange mounts, while the white men had to keep riding their tired horses every day. But driving loose horses or even leading them would slow the Indians down and perhaps rob them of that advantage. The handicaps of each party were great.

Milton knew that he had an even greater handicap than either party. He had white men. And his party was made up mostly of town-grown white men. In addition, there were a set of twin brothers who were lightly touched in the head. He wished he were riding with the Indians.

Chapter Twelve

Milton watched the Indians disappear over a slight rise, then he climbed on his horse and walked the animal slowly down the rise toward the white men. He kept his horse at a slow pace, not wanting to stir up dust for the Indians to see. Let them think that a group of whites, ignorant in the ways of the plains and the Comanche, were following them with only one scout. He was sure the Comanche scout had spotted Polo trying to keep himself concealed as he rode. They would think he was the only smart one in the group.

He rode within sight of the search party and signaled in the sign language of the Plains Indians. If no one else understood him, he hoped Polo had learned some of the ways of his mother's people.

Polo rode into view and signaled that he understood and would relay the message. The message was: The Comanche they were searching for had been sighted. The search party had been seen. They must travel with care and make plans. I tell you to wait, I want you to wait.

Milton was still angry because they did not wait for him, but had charged on like boys hot after a young girl. He rode his tired horse to the trail left by the Comanche and followed at a steady but cautious pace. He followed for two hours, and the Indians did not increase their speed. When he reached the edge of a broad patch of buffalo grass, he halted his horse. The area was large and in a slight fold of land between two low rises. It was a suspicious-looking area. He could not pin it down; nor were their signs that this was a likely ambush site. But he had lived this long because of his developed sixth sense and his training to heed it. He sat on his horse and waited for the rest of the men to catch up.

When Aguila rode up, he asked, "What do we have, amigo?"

"First, the next time I tell men to wait for me, it is for a reason. We are playing the game of death, and bad players get men killed," Milton told him bluntly. There was no friendliness in his voice.

"I am sorry, my friend. I will insist more strongly next time," Aguila said.

"I don't like what we have here. This area we are now looking over was out of my view for a good while. It looks like a good spot for a young brave to make his coup, earn his feather and a new war name," Milton told the men.

"Where would a man hide in this grass? It is too short for a man to hide in." Aguila believed what Milton told him, but it was hard to be convinced on this one.

"This area is a buffalo run. The sign is everywhere. I have seen two old shallow pits the Comanche used to spring upon the buffalo. A man can hide in such pits to spring upon another man as well," Milton told them.

"That would be suicide, eh?" Jean said, smiling.

"That is ridiculous! No one man would be stupid enough to jump an armed band as large as this one," Juan scoffed. "We are wasting time. I say we move on."

Aguila hesitated and looked at Milton. "What do you say?"

"We skirt around the area," Milton advised.

Aguila looked hard and long at the spot, as if by looking long and hard enough he would be able to see anyone hidden below the surface. "I don't know, Juan. Milton may be correct. He knows the ways of the Comanche better than any of us."

"Yes, he may be correct. And he may not. If he is wrong, we have wasted time that could be used to catch up with the Comanche," Juan said, never ready to agree when there was room for argument. "But we have among us a man whose mother's people are Comanche. We will ask him."

"This would be questioning Don Milton to his face," Aguila

said tersely. "I have said that we would take all advice from Don Milton concerning the Comanche, without question."

Aguila looked over at Milton.

The tall man shrugged his shoulders, indicating that he didn't care one way or the other what was done. All he wanted was for it to be done, and done in a hurry.

Juan saw the shrug and said, "We should ask Polo."

Aguila also shrugged his shoulders, then he ordered, "José, ask Polo to join us."

"Sí, *patrón*," José replied politely, reigning his horse around to signal for Polo.

Milton smiled. The vaqueros were using the term *patrón* when talking to Aguila; this was not lightly used by a Mexican. The men from the ranch had accepted their young mistress's man as their leader. It looked as if the saddle had been put in place and the girth tightened.

Polo rode up to the men and sat quietly, waiting patiently to be noticed, as befitted a common vaquero.

"Ah, Polo!" said Aguila. "Don Milton here, my friend and protector against savage Indians, says that a Comanche brave or two could be hiding in wait in this tall grass. That these one or two brave warriors might attack us just to prove themselves as men, great warriors. What say you of this?"

"It could be true, *patrón*. Although there are many of us, there are men such as that," Polo said politely.

"Would one or two braves be so foolish as to attack a large and well-armed party as this just to be able to wear a feather in their dirty hair?" Juan asked impatiently.

"I have heard that this is the custom, senor," Polo answered, looking from one to the other. He was indeed a breed, a mestizo, in some trouble at the moment. He did not always know just how to approach these Spanish-blooded men of quality. Polo knew that Don Juan was the type who wanted everyone who disagreed with him to be proven wrong. But he also knew the tall Yanqui had been right about most things on this trip, and he wanted to say he would follow this man's lead. This Yanqui could speak the languages of both of his mother's people, Spanish and Comanche. It was said that he could speak other languages and knew the ways and customs of many people. A man such as he would know more about these Comanche than a simple, uneducated man like himself. But Polo did not want to give a definite answer because he did not wish to agree or disagree with something of such great importance. If he were wrong at anytime. . . . The problems of a simple mestizo!

"I think Don Milton is right, but I do not know for sure," he finally said.

Milton sat his horse, an impassive, noncommittal expression on his face. He had given his advice, now it was up to them to act upon it. But whatever was done, he wished again that it would be decided upon quickly. Time was awasting.

"We should decide quickly, messieurs," Jean said, echoing Milton's sentiments. The Comanche, he is going to go from us."

"Sí! Why should men like us wait on a few ignorant savages?" asked one of the Navarro twins.

"Sí! We will take care of them ourselves, me and my little brother," said the older of the two. Even the firstborn of twins was of importance in the line of succession.

The Navarro brothers had become more and more outspoken among the men as they went along.

"That is true. What can one or two men with bow and arrows do to us?" asked Juan incredulously. For the first time he gave the Navarro brothers an appreciative look.

"*Bueno!* If that is what you wish, then we will move on through!" Aguila said. The importance of Milton's advice must be settled once and for all. "Let's move quickly."

Milton kicked his horse forward before Aguila had finished speaking. Polo rode off to the high ground on their flank. Milton did not say what he was thinking, but to him there should be only one chief, and his commands should not be questioned at every turn. Given time, these men would learn. But it would be a costly education.

Milton took the top off his canteen as he rode and poured

some of its contents into the palm of his right hand. He bathed his face, neck, and the part of his chest he could reach. He softly sang his war song. He had symbolically performed "go to water." Water was a sacred messenger to Uguwiyahi, the Great Chief above. Only fire was a more sacred messenger to the Cherokee. Milton wore a leather bag around his neck filled with *wodi,* "war paint." He seldom wore his war paint or fully performed *idigawesdi,* which lasted four days before going into battle. The more imminent the battle, the shorter the ceremony. He knew of men who had spit on their hands and wiped it over their face and chest in the act of "go to water" when there was no water. He was bypassing some of the customs of the Cherokee. His grandfather had said many times, "The old ways have wings of swift birds. They fly away or die and leave no sign."

The sea of grass stood still in the afternoon heat. Not even a wisp of wind eased the heat of the hot sun beating down upon a scorched world. Cascades of sweat ran down the men's faces and into their eyes, the salt stinging them. The backs of those who wore cotton shirts were soaking wet. They looked as if someone had poured water on them, or as if they had been in a rainstorm. Pancho suffered most of all. He was soaked from head to toe, and it seemed the hot sun was rendering all the moisture from his heavy frame. He had sweated so much that his heavy boots were filling with body liquid.

Milton rode out a hundred yards in advance of the party. His sharp eyes darted over the land in front of him, straining to pick up any alien object that didn't belong, any disturbance of the landscape. Although he rode relaxed in his saddle, every nerve in his body was strung as tight as a mountaineer's catgut fiddle string. And his taut nerves were playing the tune of danger. The animal-like instinct that had helped him survive in a world of violence for so many years now warned him to cock his long rifle and have it ready at a moment's notice.

The last man of the search party passed through the swell of land. Two young Comanche braves, who had been waiting patiently in their hot, shallow holes, rose as one. They threw back the buffalo hides that covered their holes and unleashed their arrows as they ran for safety. These two braves had answered Juan Pérez's question as to whether there were men who would endanger their lives just to wear a new feather.

Manuel González sucked in his breath as the arrow pierced the left side of his back and the sharp-flinted arrowhead severed the pulmonary artery two inches above his heart. He was a dead man before he hit the ground.

The Comanche brave who had killed Gonzalez ran to the right of the startled men. When he saw Polo he fell to one knee and shot an arrow at the approaching man. The arrow lodged high in the right side of Polo's chest. The young breed felt the searing stab of pain as the shaft drove the cutting arrowhead through the bone and muscle just above his right lung. He could feel himself falling from the saddle but could not check himself as he fell. The ear-splitting scream that was wrenched from between his clenched teeth seemed detached from him, as if it had come from another voice.

The young brave lunged for Polo's horse as it passed and swung into the saddle. With a savage cry of victory and defiance, he rode off to join his comrades.

José Hernández did not feel the cutting arrow that struck him at the base of the skull. The arrow passed between two neck vertebrae and severed the lifeline between body and brain.

The second brave let loose a second arrow a split second after the first that had killed Hernandez, showing some of the best archery any of the white men had ever seen. The arrow hit the horse Eduardo Gutiérrez was riding in the left flank and drove its sharp arrowhead deep into the bowels of the animal. The horse screamed in its agony of death and fell forward, breaking its neck as it hit the ground in a roll. The wiry Mexican horseman jumped free of the falling animal, drawing his pistol with his free hand as he fell. Always the horseman who worried about the suffering of his mount, he shot the wounded animal with his pistol. He fell behind it for cover, his rifle ready for use.

The Indian bounded off like the animal for which his band had been named, screaming out his yells of triumph. When he returned to his friends he would be honored as a brave warrior. On this day his arrows had found their mark on both a dreaded enemy and one of the horses that carried the white man into the land of the Comanche. All of this was done within the time it takes a tired dog to pant twice.

He thought the element of surprise, his speed, and the reluctance of the white men to follow when they didn't know the location of the enemy would save him. But he had not figured on the presence of a man such as Milton Hicks.

Milton had been taught from youth that when ambushed you did not stand still or run. You attacked, and you attacked with all the vigor and might you had. This sudden act usually catches the enemy totally by surprise and turns the tables on him. Milton was ready for an ambush, and he reacted accordingly.

The tall man dug his heels into the flanks of his horse and rode after the fleeing Comanche. A bloodcurdling war cry issued from the lips of the usually quiet man that both awed and sent chills down the spines of his comrades. It was not a war cry that was used to build up a man's courage to go forth and do battle, but one of utter joy and expectation of the coming clash of two warriors in a life-and-death struggle. The ancestral blood of the most warring nation of peoples in North America before the coming of the white man surged through his veins. He was being called upon to perform as he had been trained to do since his youth—to close with and kill the enemy. It was an honor to test his abilities against one of the ultimate in warriors on horseback, the Comanche.

Milton dropped the reins and let them hang loose on the pony's neck. The little pony was a war horse, and it would run straight and true for any enemy its master pointed out. Only death would deter the animal from its objective. Milton held his rifle in his left hand and drew his tomahawk. He would save his rifle for other Comanche who might be present.

The young Comanche brave heard the war cry, and the hair

at the nape of his neck rose. This was a war cry of confidence, given by an old warrior who had been victorious in battle many times. The sound made him falter, but only for an instant. He turned to meet this new adversary. The Comanche is a sad sight when unhorsed and upon the ground. He is as large as other Plains Indians, but being a mountain Indian before the coming of the horse, he was as graceful as a monkey upon the plains. His short, stocky legs were built for his once native mountain home. But like his cousin the Kiowa, once astride a horse he is transformed into one of the most graceful and majestic figures of the plains. There are no other Plains Indians, or few other North American Indians, who adapted to the horse so quickly and so well.

This young brave needed a horse. But he stood his ground, confident in his ability with the bow, for he was the best of the young braves of his band. His bow would not fail to send his arrows straight and true to their mark.

The first arrow struck and lodged in the pommel of Milton's saddle. The little pony paused slightly in stride, throwing off the aim of the young Comanche's next shot as the arrow flew past Milton. The young man should have hit with the second arrow, because he did not have time for a third shot. Milton was upon him in a few short jumps of his pony, his tomahawk raised shoulder high. The Comanche stood his ground to send another arrow. Milton gave a powerful, sweeping blow with the war ax. He did not miss, and the sharp blade of the tomahawk completely severed the top of the Comanche's head. His brain disintegrated as though it had exploded. Thousands of small gray droplets sprinkled the hot sand. The young brave fell and lay crumpled in a heap like a discarded rag doll.

Milton whirled his horse around, not to look at his kill but to look for the second warrior. He saw the brave riding off on Polo's horse. The Comanche was at too great a distance for Milton's horse to catch or his rifle to reach. He surveyed the ground around him for other hidden enemy and could find nothing amiss.

The Comanche who had gotten away on Polo's horse had

also heard the tall man's war cry. It was not the yell of any white man he had ever heard. He looked over his shoulder as his companion unloosed his two arrows. To his amazement, his friend had missed with both arrows. The white man had then closed upon his friend and killed him with a tomahawk. This was indeed a bad omen, for this was a new kind of warrior among the white men. He had much to tell his leader and his companions.

Every member of the search party had dropped from his saddle when the first arrow was shot. Only the Frenchman, Jean du Bois, had fired his rifle. He reloaded his weapon with a sheepish grin. In his haste to fire, he had missed a target of not more than thirty paces. The happy-go-lucky Frenchman would afterward turn red and bluster an excuse every time the subject of his grand miss came up. But he had nothing to be ashamed of, for he was the only one to get off a shot. With a one-shot muzzle loader, you chose your target carefully. None of the other men had a clear shot to make a sure hit.

The men rushed to where José lay and found that he would never again make music at a fiesta with his guitar. Manuel had also danced at his last fandango and chased his last senorita to the bushes along the creek banks. Eduardo sat on the ground, unhurt, his back against his dead horse. He was in the process of reloading his empty pistol. He grinned and waved a hand to Milton as the tall man rode past.

When Milton reached Polo, he dropped from his horse and looked at the wound. A faint smile crossed the lips of the young Mexican breed before he passed out in a faint. Milton drew his knife and cut Polo's shirt open. He pulled the arrow shaft out of the man's chest, covered him with his own poncho, and stood up. The arrowhead remained in Polo's chest, for most arrowheads were tied to the shaft so they would remain in the target if the shaft was pulled or fell out. Someone would have to stay behind with Polo.

Aguila walked up, followed by most of the party. He looked down at Polo. "I think this man's bravery should never be questioned by anyone in the future," Aguila said, looking Juan

Pérez straight in the eye, "even if he is a breed Kiowa-Comanche."

Juan refused comment. He knew everyone felt as Aguila did.

"What do you say now, amigo?" Aguila asked Milton, ignoring the others in the group.

"We must move on or we will not be able to keep up with the Comanche," Milton advised him.

"Agreed. We will leave two men behind with Polo and the rest of us will go," Aguila told the men.

He looked around at the men. His new role of commander of a group of men out to make war was having its effect on the onetime playboy of San Antonio. It was making him a serious-minded man. He had risen to the occasion as Milton thought he would.

"Juan Alvarez and Raphael Gonzalez, you will remain behind with Polo. We will come back this way to pick you up. If one of you can, cut out the arrowhead. If an army patrol comes this way, you will go with them and get Polo to a doctor," Aguila ordered.

The two men looked at him and then at the rest of the men. The picture of the American mountain men they had found on the trail was still fresh in their memories.

Raphael cleared his throat, "Just the two of us stay, senor?"

"I will stay with them," a man offered quickly.

Two other men stepped forward and said just as quickly, "I will stay."

The other man nodded that this was also his wish.

The thought of going on into the unknown had suddenly overwhelmed these men. They had made a quick decision that if enough stayed, it would be safer than going on and looking for a fight. They were located near a small creek that still held some water, and they could take up defensive positions.

Aguila paused for a moment and then agreed. These men were all from San Antonio, not the ranch. They were not used to the trail or a fight. And they didn't need men who were not willing to go forward on their own.

"If you are not back by this time in two days we will go back to San Antonio," Juan Alvarez told him. "We will cut the first trees we come to and make a travois for Polo."

"No, don't wait on us. Go as soon as you see that Polo can travel. But not before," Aguila told him. "You should travel in safety with your numbers."

Eight American mountain men had not traveled upon this Comanche land in safety, they thought.

"You should cauterize the wound before infection sets in and you move him," Milton told the men.

"Oh, *Madre de Dios,*" whispered one of the men. "I could not do such a thing!"

"Then bury him now and get it over with," Milton said bluntly. "You will have a dead man on your hands before you get ten miles. If he dies because you did not do the proper things, I will talk to all of you when I return to San Antonio."

Without another word, Milton walked over to where Eduardo's horse lay and skinned back some of the animal's hide. He cut off a large piece of meat from its rear quarters. Eduardo and some of the men gasped with surprise.

"A man needs fresh meat when traveling. And you can sure get hungry out on the Llano Estacado," was Milton's only comment.

Eduardo looked at his mount sadly. "I could not eat the flesh of such a noble mount as my Avispon."

The rest of the men would not take fresh meat from the dead animal.

"You men are lucky. Evidently none of you have ever been hungry," Milton told them.

Without another word he placed the meat under his saddle and swung aboard. The horse's sweat would add salt. He rode off, and the rest of the men mounted and followed. Each member of the two groups was sure that it would be the last they would see of each other. They also knew that Polo Lopez would never reach de Bexar alive.

Milton rode past the two dead men, not bothering to look their way. They were gone, and nothing could be done for

them now. They were now *unutsilunehi*, "spirits of the dead."
It was now up to the Great Chief up above to decide what
would be done with their souls.

"Wrap the bodies tightly; bury them deep," Aguila reminded the men who were staying behind. "We will send back
for the bodies later."

Aguila rode by the dead and forced himself not to look at
the men. He needed a steady hand and a clear head for what
was to come. He was jolted when he turned his head to miss
looking at the bodies of his two companions and looked instead upon the brutally slain body of the young Comanche
who had lost the top of his head to Milton's tomahawk.

Juan Pérez did not bother to look at the two dead men, but
for a different reason. To him they were nothing but mestizos,
mixed Spanish peon and Indian, and therefore of no importance.

Pancho crossed himself as he passed the men, saying a silent
prayer for all of them, as he would for any man. If the priest
was right, a prayer could intercede for their souls. If this was
not a possibility, why not pray anyway. A prayer is a small
thing to give.

Jean du Bois passed the men, a look of anger on his face.
That could have been his body lying there, and it angered him.

José Sanchez crossed himself as he passed the dead. They
were not his true friends, but he had drunk *cerveza* and tequila
with these man when they came to San Antonio. He would
drink a tequila in their honor when he returned. Ah! When he
returned, he would drink a bottle in his own honor.

For the first time on the trip, the Navarro brothers were not
laughing and giggling. They had seen the brutal death of three
men and another wounded and near death. It was a sobering
sight for most men, even for the half-crazy Navarro brothers.

Antonio Zapata quickly crossed himself and suddenly
jerked back on the reins of his horse. He turned the animal
and slowly walked it back to the men who stood beside Polo.
He would go no farther into the homeland of the Comanche.

Pablo Ruiz looked back and saw the men build a small fire.

It would be used to heat the blade of a knife red-hot to cauterize Polo's wound. He gave an involuntary shudder. He was glad it was not he who had to do this messy business. Better still, he was glad that it was not his wound that had to be cauterized.

The size of the search party was slowly decreasing. Three men had quit the party on the first day. Now two had been killed and five others remained behind with the wounded Polo. That left a grand total of fourteen men. Fourteen men riding into the heart of Comanche land. But most of these men were from the ranch that the young captive had come from, and they would rather leave their bones out on the plains and their souls to the good Virgin Mary than return to their *patrón* without his daughter.

But all were uneasy. All except the tall Milton Hicks, who seemed to live for adventure and violence. What about this tall man, the men thought? He had not stepped down and taken what was left of the scalp of the Comanche he had killed. But he had stopped and looked long into the dead man's face. To these men he was a weird one. Weird, but brave beyond belief. They did not know that the Cherokee believed that a man who has been scalped could not enter the land of the Great One. Milton would never take a scalp unless he hated the man.

The men rode slowly, deep in thought. The stories of large parties going into the Llano Estacado, never to be heard of again, preyed heavily upon their minds. Soon they would leave the rough terrain and turn west to climb the caprock and enter the dreaded land of the Comanche, the Llano Estacado.

Chapter Thirteen

The Comanche raiding party stopped long before dark and made camp. Another mule was killed and cooked over an open fire.

Young Josephine sat quietly, resigned to the fact that she might never see her family again—at least not in this world. All the hysteria and panic she had experienced when the Comanche band first fell upon her had long since passed. She found that as time passed these savage red men meant her no immediate bodily harm. None of them had raped her, which she had been told all her life would happen if she was ever captured by Indians. Nor had she been beaten. She had been left pretty much alone when they found that she could not cook. It was amazing to them to find a woman who could not accomplish the simple chore of cooking. Every Comanche girl could cook, and every woman had become an expert by the time she was grown. In their eyes she was not a young girl but a grown woman. The only time she had been struck was when she was given a command and she did not obey quickly enough. All the young braves and some of the older ones could speak Spanish, and she had no difficulty understanding the orders she was given. After the first slap against her head, she began to move more quickly at a given command.

Her hopes of rescue rose when she found that they were being followed by a rescue party of white men. But they began to drop hour after hour when the rescue party did not come to rescue her. The white men should attack the red men. They had only two rifles between them. Little did she know that the Comanche would kill her before they gave her up. She was nothing more than a captive slave of war, a woman at that, and they would kill her as easily as they killed a rabbit for the pot. If at a later time she was taken to the tent of a young brave as his wife, then she would no longer be treated as a slave or an alien white person. These same men who would now kill her would then fight to the death to protect her life along with that of the other women of their tribe. As an adopted member of the tribe, she would no longer be considered a member of a subrace, which the Comanche considered all other people to be.

Josephine looked up from where she sat and her hopes rose again. Off in the distance she could see a man standing on a small rise of land in full view of the Indians. She was going to be saved!

The Indians talked excitedly and pointed in his direction. The young brave who had ambushed the white men's party and escaped told his comrades that this was the man who had killed their friend.

"He is truly a warrior of much experience," the young man told them. "His cry is that of a man who is sure of his ability to kill all who stand in his way. From this one cry, although I am young, I knew I had heard the cry of victory of an old warrior who is sure of his kill even before his act."

"He is truly that good?" one asked.

"He is," the first young warrior said in admiration.

"And Buffalo's Tail's arrows flew past him as if there was a shield to protect him?" another asked.

"Ah, that is true," the first one replied. "I saw it with my own eyes."

"You will never be called a *pivi* by anyone," said another young warrior.

The Comanche calls a man a *pivi*, "elder sister," when he runs from a fight.

The chief of the party, Run-to-water, stood to one side, but he heard the talk of his warriors. He had seen great warriors before, and as all warriors knew, every warrior can die, be they great or small. It may even be his time to die like a warrior. If so, then so be it. A Comanche did not lose much sleep over that proposition.

The grizzled old *puhakut*, "medicine man," stood looking at the tall man on the hill. He knew of the mortality of a man, whether or not he was a warrior. But for good measure, he slipped his rattle from the folds of his clothes and shook it at the man on the hill. He wished his *yuane*, "bull roarer," was not back at the main camp.

The Comanche were dressed in their best now that they might have to go to battle. Old clothes were worn for everyday use and traveling, but a warrior wore his best when going into battle. If he were killed, he should not enter the camp of the afterworld beyond the sun as a beggar. And a Comanche always put on his best just before entering camp when returning from a trip.

The wardrobe of the Comanche was made from things adapted from his life on the plains. His short bow was made from the bois d'arc, hickory, ash, ironwood, or any other hardwood found along the banks of streams or water holes. Bow strings were made of sinew from a tendon alongside the backbone of a buffalo bull or antelope. Arrows were made from any good hardwood, though young shoots of the dogwood were preferred. The feathers could be used from any bird except the crow, which had no *puha*, "power." And *puha* was the most important thing to a Comanche. He would gladly die to gain *puha*. The shields, about two feet in diameter, were made of buffalo bull hide. Two hides were sewn together, with feathers, hair, or animal fur between them to help stop arrows or bullets.

Each warrior wore a medicine bag around his neck. The bag contained material substance that served as a medium for consultation with a guardian spirit. Sweet grass, herbs, a deer's tail, a bird's claw, small stones, and the hides of animals were found in the bag. Each item had a use for the wearer. The sweet grass was protective. The herbs had healing power, and the bird's claw inspired dash and courage. The stones brought good health and long life since they did not wear out. The

small balls from a buffalo's stomach not only added great
strength but also made one invincible in battle. The skin from
animals helped to give the warrior the animals' most noted
characteristic: speed, strength, courage, and stamina.

A warrior wore a breechclout, not for modesty's sake but
because it magically protected his male organs. His buckskin
leggings extended from hip to ankle, were usually decorated
with fringes, and were attached at the top with a waist belt.
The moccasins had buckskin uppers with a seam down the
heel and a sole of buffalo hide. A buffalo robe was a regular
part of the wardrobe to be carried winter or summer. The war
bonnet was a skullcap around which feathers drooped or
spread backward. When not being worn, it was kept in a
parafleche cylinder called a *tunawaws,* which also contained
war paint. Another parafleche bag, called an *awyaut,* was used
for carrying pemmican.

Milton stood on the slight rise in plain view of the men
below and watched them in the failing light. Let them see him.
Let them know that he was not afraid, and that he would
follow. Before long they would know that he would follow
them as long as they had the girl or he was alive.

Only two short miles separated them, but it might as well
have been 2,000. He knew that the girl's life would be forfeit if
they boldly attacked the Comanche camp. If the Comanche
decided to fight on their own accord, then the girl's life would
be saved no matter who won. But if the white men pushed the
Comanche into a fight, they would kill the girl out of anger.
Milton knew that before they would let the captive be taken
back, they would slit her throat. A woman's life, even a Comanche woman, meant little to a Comanche warrior if he had
to decide between her and honor. In his society a man could
kill his wife in anger and no one would say a thing.

No, Milton and the white men must play a dangerous game
of cat and mouse until the Indians either made a mistake or
decided to stand and fight. But every mile they went, they
would be leading the white men deeper into the plains. If the
raiding party met up with a hunting or war party of either

Comanche or Kiowa, the rescue party would not only lose the
girl but would suffer another loss—that of their own lives.
There were no prisoners of war among most Indian tribes for
the simple reason that they had no prisons in which to hold
them, and no extra food with which to sustain them. Since the
Comanche gave no quarter, he asked for none in return.

Milton had heard white men tell of capturing a Comanche,
who, when he had been set free, was so relieved at not being
killed that he cried. This was not so. The brave had cried
because he was ashamed. A Comanche refused to surrender,
and when pressed beyond an honorable escape, he would dis-
mount, throw away his moccasins as a token never to retreat,
and fight to resist as long as his strength lasted. Often a Comanche would kill himself rather than be taken prisoner. The
Comanche made an extra effort never to be captured by the
Mexicans when the Indians learned that the white men sometimes hanged Indians taken prisoner. Death by strangulation
was the most dreaded form for a Comanche, for they believed
the spirit of man came out of his mouth when he died. Next
was the fear of death in the dark away from home, for the
spirit that left the body in the dark would forever wander in
darkness in its search for the afterworld beyond the sun.

Milton searched his mind for a way to attack the Comanche.
They were still on the eastern edge of the Llano, and tomorrow or the next day the Indians would head directly into the
high plains. Then an ambush by the white men would be next
to impossible. The land would be so level that it would be
possible to see a man for miles. And they would be in grass so
short it would hide no one except a Comanche.

He walked back to his own camp.

José Sanchez and Eduardo Gutierrez were cooking the antelope Milton happened upon that afternoon. The fire made of
dried buffalo chips was blue-flame hot. The Indians had
learned centuries ago that dried animal dung made cleaner,
hotter fire than wood.

The white men didn't have to worry about the Indians seeing their fire. The Comanche not only knew their camp's loca-

tion but the location of every man in it. The white men would have to be especially watchful at daylight the next morning, for the Comanche loved to attack as the sun rose.

Milton squatted Indian fashion just outside the circle of men and unwrapped the piece of horsemeat he had taken from Eduardo's horse. He would save his share of the fresher antelope for another time. With a short wooden handle he always carried, he stuck the meat through a sharpened pointed iron rod. Then he went to the fire to cook the meat.

"Senor, I speak with respect, but I couldn't force myself to eat the meat of a horse," said Eduardo, the vaquero and lover of horses.

Milton grunted that he understood. A vaquero loved his horse as much as a member of his family. A man such as he, who lived a catch-as-catch-can existence, had long ago found that one does not always question the fare he is about to partake of. There were very few things that were taboo for a Cherokee when it came to food. The white man had no real taboos save those dictated by his religion. Milton ate anything that would sustain life. The Comanche would not eat dog. By tradition a dog ate an old woman many years ago, and no Comanche would eat the descendants of an animal that had eaten one of his ancestors. The Comanche refused to kill a coyote, not because it was cousin to the dog, but because the coyote was a trickster, a demigod, and had medicine.

He let the meat sear on the outside and then began to eat. He also knew, as all men of the woods knew, that the greatest nourishment came from meat that did not have all of the blood cooked from it. And he was going to need all the nourishment he could get during the next few days.

"I know I couldn't eat horsemeat," Juan Pérez said.

Milton shrugged his shoulders noncommittally.

"Not even if I were real hungry," Juan added.

"What is real hunger?" Milton asked, looking Pérez in the eye.

"I don't know," Juan admitted.

"Your ancestors, the conquistadors, they knew. They would

and did eat their horses to survive. They would and did eat their enemy to survive, with their monk's blessings," Milton told him. "There weren't many things that stopped the Spanish conquistadors."

Juan turned pale and nearly gagged on the piece of meat he had just placed in his mouth. He spit it out and looked at Milton. Milton was talking about his ancestors, but he dared not say anything. The arrogant Yanqui had a combative look about him at the moment.

Milton cut hot slivers of meat with his razor-sharp knife.

"I say we have come far enough," Juan said, the color returning to his face. "We are now at the very edge of the Llano Estacado. Comanche country for sure."

"Anything west of San Antonio de Bexar is Comanche country," Jean told him. "And many times even east of de Bexar."

"Yes, yes. It is true that once you leave the city limits you are in Comanche country. Or Lipan, or Mescalero, or some other red devil's country. But now! Whew! We must indeed be fools," Juan complained, throwing his uneaten food into the fire. "Senor Hicks says that tomorrow the Comanche may turn more westwardly into the Llano. I say that we have gone far enough. We cannot get to the girl. To try would cost her her life. I think we should go home."

"And I," agreed Pablo Ruiz.

"Juan! Pablo! We must go on! We must rescue the daughter of Don Raul. I have vowed that I would not return without her," Aguila told his comrades. "We must do those things for him that he cannot do for himself. If he and his sons were here they would not turn back."

"That is probably true. Blood is thicker than water," Juan Pérez said, standing up and finishing the rest of his coffee. "But Don Raul is a smart and reasonable man. He has others in his family who need him. And we also. I think we have gone far enough into the Llano. It is foolish to go further."

"Then you call me a foolish man, for I will continue," Aguila told him defiantly.

"But, Aguila, it is more than foolish. Look what we have lost to these savages already, and we will lose more," Pablo said earnestly. "Three good men are lost already. And we are very fortunate. But for the grace of God, man, it will be more if we go into the Llano Estacado! No, I think Juan is right! We should go back."

"Sí! We have lost three men, and the Comanche only one! There are also seventeen of them and thirteen of us," Juan added. "If they are joined by another band, we are lost."

"We can't quit now," Aguila told them. "Look! Over that small rise, not more than two miles away, the girl we came for is waiting for us. She knows that the brave men of her people have come to save her. We cannot go and tell Raul Rodriguez that we were so close to his daughter yet did nothing. At least I cannot, and will not."

"We can do nothing, don't you understand? If we try, the Comanche will kill her," Juan told him. He kicked dirt into the fire. He wanted to scream out his arguments, but he would not belittle himself in front of the peons and this Yanqui. And the knowledge that the Comanche were so close tended to subdue the volume of his voice.

"But look, amigos! Our good scout, Don Milton, has told us that the Comanche have only two rifles among them," Aguila told the men.

"It wasn't the rifles that killed our three men," said Juan. He was not going to be sucked into the old belief that one-shot, muzzle-loading rifles were superior to bows and arrows. He had to admit that the only rifle here for true long-range, accurate shooting was the one carried by Milton Hicks.

"But look, we are thirteen men, each with a rifle, and most of us carry two pistols. Look at the firepower we have. It would take many to stand against us," Aguila argued, hoping that he could convince the men to stay with him.

"Just two rifles?" asked Pablo. "The number could be greater. Men have been known to be wrong. Even Yanquis."

"And some men have been known to be born fools and die

fools," Milton said quietly, making no further effort to confront the Mexican.

Pablo turned red-faced but held his tongue. Pablo would not attack Milton Hicks even if the tall man was naked and chained to the mast of a sinking ship. He would rather attack the Comanche bare-handed, he thought.

Everyone sat for an uncomfortable minute.

"I do not say that Don Milton is wrong," said Juan, "but he may be wrong in leading us into the Llano. We may get killed. You will always take his advice until we are led into a large band of these red savages."

"No, Milton is not leading us anywhere. He is scouting for us. We go on our own will," Aguila reminded him.

"That is true. I admit my mistake," Juan acknowledged.

"We must trust his knowledge of the ways of the Comanche, and trust his judgment. He knows more about the Comanche than all of us. We go on," Aguila told them. There was no backing down in his voice.

"He is correct, Juan. The Yanqui knows more than any of us," Pablo added, trying to rectify his earlier mistake. "We must follow his lead or we will certainly be lost."

"And, senors, Aguila is correct. I don't lead anyone where they do not wish to go," Milton said quietly. "I also suggest that if you wish to fight, we should do so with the Comanche, not with each other."

Juan finished his meat and stood up, wiping the blade of his knife on his pants leg. He knew that Aguila would not give up. And he and the rest of the men were bound to him. None of them could return without him or Raul's daughter. None of the men of quality, that is. The breeds and men of the alley could do as they wished. They were not men of honor. But the men of quality were bound to a code they must live by, come death or Comanche. The Mexican was tied to many of the traditions of the Spanish, and a man of proud heritage would gladly face death before dishonor. And Juan Pérez was proud. No, if any of them left the search party with Raul Rodriguez's daughter so close, they would do so without honor. This he would not do.

He looked in the direction of the Comanche camp. A dim glow of the Indians' fire could be seen reflected on the surface of the crystal-clear sky. This would be the last day some of them would live to see such a sky. "We must cut down their number some way," Juan grumbled. "If they do not meet another band soon, they will turn and fight us alone. It is against the custom of the Comanche to let white men get very far into their country. They will not let an enemy find their main camp with the women and children, or discover their secret water holes."

He looked around at the men and gave a wry smile, "See, amigos? I, Juan Pérez, also know a little about the Comanche."

The Navarro brothers sat to one side of the men, giggling and pushing each other playfully as usual. Ricardo, the firstborn of the two, looked up from their play. "My brother, Rocco, and me, we will cut down the odds of these bandits."

"Ha! You make me laugh!" Juan said in disgust.

"Do not laugh, Don Juan," said Rocco the younger, using the familiar term of *Don* instead of *Patrón*, as befit someone of his own station. "If my brother, Ricardo, says we will do this thing, then, senors, it is as good as done."

"These are Comanche warriors you are talking about," Aguila reminded the brothers. "They are not to play with. And how do you expect to lower their number?"

"Yes! You will play games with them and make them laugh themselves to death. Is that your plan?" Juan asked in his most sarcastic manner.

"No, senors. My brother, Rocco, and I are Mescalero from our father's people," Ricardo told them. "We will slip upon these Comanche horse thieves in the dark and dispatch them with our knives. Eh, little brother?"

"Sí, big brother, that is for true."

"Your father, the great Mescalero warrior. I must laugh at the remark. He is only part Mescalero, and he has lost all of it in the cantinas and whorehouses of San Antonio," Pablo said with disgust. He was talking to peons now, and he knew how to deal with them. "He is so little of a man that he lets his wife whore for him to keep him in tequila. You *niños* know no more about fighting Comanche than he does about beating someone besides a woman. You fight in the alleys of the town, usually two of you against one who is smaller. This is a different fight, and a different alley. You had better stick to your own kind."

"You do not need to talk such things about our mother," Rocco objected.

Milton felt the same. A man of any real substance does not talk about women in such a manner.

"We will cut their number in half before the sun rises. I, Ricardo Navarro, have said so. And I also say so for my little brother, Rocco Navarro," Ricardo told them defiantly.

"For the love of a pig's ass, stop repeating your names," complained Juan.

Aguila threw his hands up into the air and cast his eyes skyward. He looked at Milton and could see the big man in the dim firelight shake his head. Of course Milton was right. These two young fools would only get themselves killed. "I order everyone to remain in camp, except Senor Hicks. He will decide for himself what he must do to keep in check with the Comanche."

"Senors! I, Ricardo Nava . . . uh, me and my little brother, we will rid this country of ours of many Comanche on this one pleasant evening," Ricardo told them, stuttering as he tried not to repeat his and his brother's names. "The stealth and bravery and ability of the Mescalero Apache are well known by all! Even the Comanche."

"Yes, but you are not true Mescalero. And a Mescalero will lose out in every encounter with the Comanche," Pablo said in a disgusted voice.

"You will remain in camp—both of you—and that is an order," Aguila told them sternly. Then he turned to Juan and Pablo. "I say again that I will not return to San Antonio. I have spoken. That is final."

Juan shrugged his shoulders, and Pablo remained silent.

Milton glanced at the Navarro brothers. They thought like all whites, or breeds who were raised in white towns. Rid their country of all red devils. Who in the hell did they think this country belonged to in the first place? He paused a moment in his thinking. To those who are strong enough to hold it, he had answered his own question. It was a sad thought, but it was true in this world. History had confirmed it. For the average man power came before ideology and theology. It had been proven so here today. It had been proven so since recorded history. He placed his huge knife in its sheath and went to rest for a few hours.

A lone coyote howled its defiance of the men who were intruding in its domain. Or was it calling a mate?

Chapter Fourteen

Milton's eyes came open and he stared at the clear, black sky, studded with bright stars, above him. The stars have a brilliance when viewed from the plains that is seen in no other region. His razor-sharp sixth sense for survival registered the uneasiness of danger. He lay a moment, trying to define the signals that were being sent to his frontier-educated brain. The old adage that a man lived by his wits in this hostile country was not something one said just for the benefit of the people back east in the cities. More than one man had perished because he hadn't learned to listen to the messages his animal instincts sent him in times of danger.

He suddenly rose and walked over to where Aguila lay. "Aguila, we are without guards," he said softly. He knew without bothering to check.

Without a word Aguila got to his feet and went with Milton to check the guard. No one could be found. The Mexican looked up at the stars. He was a man of the trail and could tell both direction and time by the heavenly bodies as well as any man. "The Navarro brothers should be on guard."

Milton grunted.

"Maybe they took their horses and rode to the Comanche camp," said Aguila.

"No horses left this camp," Milton informed him.

"Those little sons-of-a-donkey! I told them to remain in camp! I forbade them to have an encounter with the Indians!" Aguila growled. There was anger in his voice, mixed with the knowledge that he was not in complete control.

"After what was said to them by the other men, even they had no choice," Milton told him.

Aguila went around to each man and shook him awake. Ricardo's and Rocco's blankets were empty. Their weapons were also missing.

A new guard was posted and the fire built up. Eduardo put a pot of coffee on the fire. The stars declared the time to be an hour and half before dawn. The men shivered in the predawn chill that comes on the early wave of dawn on the prairie. The long, hard days of travel with little rest and food, the constant strain of being in Comanche country and following hostile Indians, had begun to wear on the men and made them edgy.

"Those young fools. I told you we should not have brought them with us," growled Juan.

"It is known by everyone that they are a little touched in the head," Pablo added. *"Loco en la cabeza."*

"They are more than a little. Both of them have passed the point of any sanity," Juan said. He made a face when his lips touched the tin cup of hot coffee.

"And you, my friend, and my friend Pablo, have done much to drive them to do something they may regret," Aguila told both of them.

"I tell no man to do anything he doesn't want to do," Juan said in the smug voice of a man of position.

"You are wrong, Juan. Other people, even peons, also have pride. You are not the only one who is a vain ass at times," Aguila informed him. He didn't bother to soften his words or the tone of his voice.

"I didn't tell them to do anything," Juan returned.

"I certainly didn't tell them what to do," Pablo told Aguila. He didn't know what the two young fools were up to, but he didn't want to be held responsible for any of it.

"What is done is done," Aguila said curtly. The problems of command were beginning to take their toll on the young Mexican, making him as short-tempered as the rest.

Pancho looked long and hard at the two men, Juan and Pablo, in the firelight. No one, not even the so-called "men of quality," would force himself upon Aguila. Not as long as he was alive. Juan and Pablo knew this to be true, and they understood Pancho's look. Pancho was only one step up from a common peon in their eyes, but he was a powerful man in de Bexar regardless of his status. All of Aguila's father's old friends were also friends of Aguila. And when one was a friend to the Guerra family, one was a friend to Pancho Amador. There was also this tall Yanqui, Milton Hicks. Aguila was in possession of some strong friends. If a Mexican understood nothing else, he understood power and strength.

The fat man pulled out his knife and cut off a large piece of the meat that had been cooked the previous evening. When there was nothing else he could do, he could always eat. Pancho's large girth was visible proof that he had felt that way for many years.

Milton walked away from the camp and sat with his back to the open fire, facing the direction of the Comanche camp. The next action would come from that camp. There was no doubt about the fate of the Navarro brothers. Not in his mind. It was only a matter of time before they were caught. He sat for a moment with his eyes closed before opening them to restore his night vision. The men sitting around the fire were fools, because light destroys one's night vision.

The yellow glow of a campfire began to shine above the top of the rise in the ground that separated the two camps. Milton knew that the Navarro brothers were no longer free men. They were now captives of the Comanche, along with the girl they were supposed to have freed from captivity. But their fate would be much worse than that of the young Josephine.

A sudden scream broke the predawn silence. Then another pierced the air. The screams came from the throats of two different men, but the sound was the same—the screams of dying souls. These screams tore into the guts of so-called civilized men, especially when they were made by their own kind. It made lesser men sick to the pit of their stomachs.

The white men in the camp stood bolt upright and crossed themselves. Gasps of fear and amazement came from most of them. For those who had never heard a tortured soul in its climactic throes of death, the sound was inhuman. That last defiant cry against the brutal passage into the unknown journey of death came strongly and in anger even from the weakest of men.

After Milton heard the screams he relaxed, for he now knew the fate of the Navarro brothers. He knew also that these screams were the sounds of death and that there was nothing that could be done for the brothers. Except kill them and put them out of their misery, and that would be impossible.

Milton filled his clay pipe and indulged himself in a smoke. He felt no real sympathy for the Navarro brothers. It was not that he was more savage than civilized; he simply felt they were getting what they deserved. Both men were fools, and fools didn't live long in Comanche country, or anyplace else where a man must live by intelligence and wits. To his way of thinking, they were receiving just punishment for leaving a sleeping camp unguarded in the middle of hostile country. It was best that they died now before they got someone killed by their stupidity. He had been hardened to these screams when he was a young warrior fighting with Jackson against the Creek Red Sticks. That time the torture had been performed by civilized white men against red men.

Aguila walked over to Milton and asked the unnecessary question, "The Navarro brothers?"

Milton didn't bother to answer.

"Holy Mother of God!" breathed Pancho.

"May the Saints preserve their souls," Jean du Bois whispered, crossing himself. There was a strained look on his normally pleasant face.

Juan, followed by Pablo, walked over to join Milton and Aguila. *"Mi Dios!"* he said. "Is there nothing we can do?"

Milton thought it was a stupid question.

"I know of nothing," Aguila told him in a strained voice.

The Navarro brothers were no-good fools and alley trash, but they were fellow human beings, thought Milton. They were now being tortured in what some would call an inhuman manner. But it was not inhuman at all. One could only be tortured by one's fellowman. Torture is not of the animal kingdom.

"Can't our half-breed Indian here do something?" Pablo Ruiz asked.

"You had better take care of yourself. I am worse than the Comanche," Milton told him easily. He could feel the eyes of all the men on him. It didn't matter what these men thought of him, for he would do what he thought best. But he asked anyway. "What would you have me do?"

Juan nearly shouted out an answer. "You could slip up close to the Comanche camp and shoot both of them with your rifle. It would at least get them out of their misery."

"We can't just stand here. We should do something, and you're the only one who would have a chance," Pablo said.

Milton knocked the fire from his pipe and said quietly in the mild-mannered voice that so frustrated his companions at times, "I may be lucky enough to get in one shot, but it is doubtful if I would live long enough to get in a second one if I tarried. I am not ready to join Asgaya Galulati upon the Sky Rock—and certainly not for a couple of damned fools like those two."

He looked around at the other men in the pale light of dawn and asked, "Who are you feeling sorry for? Those poor souls you were so contemptuous of a few hours ago, or yourselves? And who among you is willing to go with me to hold a second rifle so I may have time to fire a second shot?"

There was no answer from any of the men.

"Direct your guilt and anger at someone else, not me," Milton told them. Without another word, the tall man walked back to his saddle and lay down.

"The bloodless son-of-a-goat. Does he not have feelings like other men? Does he not feel for anyone except Milton Hicks?" Pablo asked under his breath. He gave another shudder at the sound of another agonized scream.

"He has none. He would not mourn for his own brother," Juan growled.

"Sí, that must be so," agreed Pablo.

All of this was said in whispers. None wished the tall man to overhear.

Indignation arose in Aguila, and he felt he must defend his friend. He knew that Milton was already asleep, having emptied his mind of that which he could not control. The big man would not even hear the agonizing screams that came from the Comanche camp. While the big Yanqui lay and slept, the rest of the camp would sit in gut-twisting agony. Aguila understood. Milton was a practical man. The Mexican knew that Milton would go and try to save the worthless lives of the Navarro brothers if he thought he could. But young Josephine's life was also at stake.

"My friends, you do Milton Hicks an injustice. I believe all of you know this. He would risk his life for anyone of us if he thought it worth the cost to do so. He is risking his life for a girl he does not even know. Can we all say the same? We all know the girl's father very well. He is a powerful man in Mexico. We are men of quality who must try to save the child of another man of quality," Aguila said, looking around at the men. "Some came on this trip because they are vaqueros of the ranch and must try to save the daughter of their patrón. Others came because they thought it might be a good adventure, and to gain the favor of men of quality. But not Milton Hicks. He came because I, his friend, asked him to come. And also because he does not wish to see someone taken against his will. Is this a man of no feeling?"

When he had finished, Aguila returned to the fire and squatted down to look into the flames. He had not bothered to tell them that Milton had also come along because he was a man of the gun and would not pass up any chance to gain glory for himself in battle.

The rest of the men joined him by the fire. No one said anything. They knew their friend had spoken the truth. This Yanqui was a strange one to them, as were most gringos. They did not understand him, as they didn't most gringos. When men do not understand another man, they usually react against him more in defense of their own ignorance than anything else. Maybe they should hold their tongues.

A scream rolled across the top of a hill. They wished the victims could hold their tongues. The screams sent chills down the spines of the silent men. All could imagine what it would be like if it were they. Nearly imagine, but not quite. Was the big man right? Did they shudder only because they imagined it could be them, and they had no real feelings for the Navarro brothers?

The sun peaked over the edge of the waking world to find the men of the search party with haggard, drawn, ashen faces. It was as if they had also endured the torture. They had suffered greatly. Not physically, but mentally. And this night would live in their memories for the rest of their lives.

Chapter Fifteen

The Comanche were experts at slow-death torture, and it was midday before the last Navarro brother died. Not that the Comanche tortured often, but torture is an act that once learned is not easily forgotten. Exaggerated accounts of Comanche, Kiowa, and Apache tortures came from a scared frontier, but only a few actual accounts were documented. There were more known and recorded atrocities committed by the white man against the red man. And it was the white man who captured the red man to be used or sold as slaves, not the other way around.

The Comanche were ready to leave as soon as the spirits of the two men had departed. They jumped astride their horses and the younger braves rode in circles around their camp, shouting defiant cries against a world that was not their own. And cries of anger against the white interlopers who dared to cross their land.

Two young braves rode straight toward the white men who had stopped on top of the rise of land and watched them. They did not pull in their mounts until they were 400 yards from the line of white men. From there the two braves sat their horses and shook their war lances at their enemies. Milton noticed that one of the horses had until the previous day belonged to Polo Lopez. If the young Comanche brave who had taken that horse lived very long, he would become an outstanding warrior.

Four of the white men dropped from their horses and to their knees with their muskets and began firing at the two

Indians. The distance was great even for a good marksmen
with a good, long rifle.

The two young Comanche gave wild yelps that sounded as
if they were laughing at the white men's poor marksmanship.
The warrior riding Polo's horse pulled hard on the reins and
his horse reared on hind legs, whirling around at the same
time. Milton was glad that Polo was not present to see his
favorite horse forced to do maneuvers he was not trained to
perform.

"Why don't you shoot with your long rifle?" asked Juan.

"Let them think all of us have muskets to shoot at them
with," Milton answered. He grinned and said, "I just might
cook up a surprise for them."

The two Indians rode back to their friends in a display of
horsemanship the white men could not help admiring, however grudgingly.

Milton watched in admiration as the two men displayed
their skills. To him the Mexican horsemen were among the
best he had ever seen. But neither the Mexican nor anyone
else could compare with the Comanche of the Great Plains of
North America.

"Look, messieurs! The Comanche has only had the horse for
a few generations, and yet there are few others who can touch
him in horsemanship," Jean du Bois said in admiration.
"These Comanche are in truth the Tartars of the plains."

"That is true. They are magnificent horsemen. The best,"
agreed José Sanchez, vaquero of the Rodriguez hacienda and
an excellent horseman in his own right. It was no mean com-
pliment for one horseman to give to another.

"They are dirty savages and horse thieves," growled Juan
Pérez. He would not grant the red man one word of admiration.

When the two Indians rejoined their friends, the group trot-
ted off, still traveling north by northwest. The captured horses
and mules were tied together in separate strings of five each
and were being led now that there was a threat of white men
following.

A mule was led by one of the subchiefs of the raiding party. On the back of the mount was the small figure of Josephine. Every man, woman, and child in a band of Comanche had his or her own horse to ride. Warriors rode only stallions or geldings. Women and children rode mares. Mules were used only for pack animals, or for captives to ride.

Josephine rode with her head bowed, for she had also endured the long night. For her it had been a firsthand observance. There was a helpless look of despair on her once lovely face. The pink color of youth had left her cheeks, now red and swollen from the effects of the hot sun and the wind. Her lips were drawn together in a pinched manner, making her to look fifteen years older than her tender fourteen years. In the depths of her eyes were mirrored the horrors of that long, terrible night. The brutal death of the Navarro brothers had been seared on her soul forever. For years to come she would awaken in the middle of the night in a cold, hysterical sweat to the screaming of the two men. Her only hope of rescue lay in the handful of white men who followed. But were they enough to rescue her from these savages?

Without a word Milton kicked his horse forward to follow the Comanche. Unknown to Josephine, this man was her only hope.

The other men followed.

Aguila rode forward, his eyes, like those of the rest of the men, straining to make out what he would soon come upon in the deserted Indian camp.

The white men rode into the deserted camp, where they found the body of only one of the Navarro brothers. He was staked spread-eagle in the middle of the camp, the bones from the dead mule used as stakes. The rawhide thongs that held his feet and arms had drawn tight as they dried and cut to the bone. The skeleton of the mule, the hide rolled beside it, and the cold campfire were the only evidence of anything else in camp.

None of the men could tell which of the Navarro brothers they had found. Empty, bloody sockets where eyes had once been stared up at the cloudless sky. His entire scalp had been removed, and the white bone of his skull had dried in the hot sun. His stomach had been cut from breastbone to pelvis, and a buffalo-dung fire had burnt the cavity hollow. He had been castrated, the Comanche way of telling the white men that his seed would never sire children who would encroach upon their land.

"God! May the Savior and Father have mercy upon his poor, tortured soul!" prayed Pancho.

"Those wretched pigs! May their fathers sire only dogs and all their mothers become sterile!" growled Juan.

"These savages! They must all be killed! All of them must be killed! Every man, woman, and child! All! And driven from our land!" cried Pablo.

"How could men do this to other men?" asked Juan, pain filling his voice. This could also happen to him on this trip. The thought was enough to anger and scare anyone.

"Only heathens! Heathens did this! Heathen savages who are more animal than human!" cried Pablo.

Milton sat his horse and listened to the pronouncements of death and destruction being wished upon the entire red race. He listened to these pious, Christian white men call the red men savages and then in the same breath say that all Indians, including women and children, should be killed or driven from the face of the earth. He smiled a bitter smile to himself.

"Have you ever heard of the way you Spanish and Mexicans have treated entire nations of red men here in this new land, which belonged first to the red man?" Milton asked. There was acid in his quiet voice. "Read and listen, and find out before you condemn anyone. I fought with the white Americans in a war.

"In our fight against the Creek nation, when Indians were killed or captured white men under the American General Jackson would cut the testicle bag off them to make a scrotum tobacco pouch. A number of white men had tobacco pouches made of women's breasts, their nipples dried and used as the bottom of the bags. Then, in the next breath, they called themselves Christians and lovers of their fellowman.

"At least the Comanche do not call themselves what they are not and say it is wrong for others to do those same things they do. You never hear an Indian say that acts of man against man is an act against God. If they believed what they did was an act against God and nature, no Indian would do these things. Never!"

The white men sat their horses, unable to speak.

"Where is the other body?" asked Aguila, breaking the trance of horror under which the men had fallen.

Milton rode to the mule hide and stepped from his horse. He drew his knife and cut the thongs that held it together. The hot sun had drawn the green mule hide drum-tight. Inside was the crushed body of one of the Navarro brothers.

"The bloody heathens!" Juan screamed in anger. "May they all, every last soul, burn in eternal damnation!"

Aguila shook his head slowly, a sick look on his face.

"No one can ever defend the red man to me after this," Pablo shouted without thinking.

Milton looked at the men in the early-morning light. He was one who would and could defend his red brother. His face remained expressionless, but there was a look of anger and contempt in his pale blue eyes that spoke louder and clearer than any words. He did not hate these men. To him hate was a waste of time.

Very quietly and slowly he said, "It is hard to believe these things I hear you speak. You say this after what the white men from Europe have done to entire Indian nations. You speak this way after the white man has slowly stolen the red man's land. After all of this, you still condemn the red man for wanting to protect his own people? You call the Comanche a heathen, then you condemn him to the hell of your God. A Comanche will kill you as a warrior, but he would never wish you to be punished for eternity by God. You say all of this, you do all of this—you use the name of God to do all of this—and

still you call yourselves peace-loving, forgiving Christians?
Men of God?"

The tall man was closer to shouting than he had been since
he was a young boy. He looked each man directly in his eyes
before each dropped his lids. "Curse them in anger as warriors
if you will. I will curse with you. But let me not hear any
more of this calling them savages and heathens, or I will show
you what savage really is."

The tall Yanqui breed did not wait to hear the reaction of
these men. He knew they would neither offer him violence
nor defy him to his face. He would not know, nor would he
care, what these men said of him when he left their presence.

Milton rode off from the men and stopped his horse, waiting
to see what they were going to do. He sat and watched the
Comanche ride off as if they hadn't a care in the world or a
need to hurry. The Comanche might not need to hurry, but
the rescue party did if it was going to keep up with them.

Sitting patiently on his horse, he looked back at the men and
waited. The thoughts of a moment ago had already left his
mind. Another matter needed his immediate attention. There
was one and only one pressing purpose for his presence here
at the moment. That was to rescue the young Josephine from
her captors. He was not here to kill or punish the Comanche.
To his way of thinking, they had done no wrong. They had
raided an enemy and had ridden off with the spoils of victory.

It was the white man who was encroaching upon the land of
the Comanche not the other way around. The white man's law
did not concern the Comanche. A man must do what he thinks
is the thing for him to do. Making attacks upon the white men
on the edge of their civilization seemed the thing to do as far as
the Comanche was concerned. Milton could not condemn a
man for that. He might kill him, but he wasn't going to say the
man was wrong.

The men in the search party were grouped together in conference. This was as far as some of them would go on this
rescue mission.

"I go no further," Juan told Aguila. "There is no hope of

stopping them now. They will head into the heart of the Llano
Estacado and we will lose all. To depend upon them to make a
mistake is a foolish idea. We could follow them all the way to
the salt flats of El Paso del Norte, or to Taos, and still not
catch them. I will go no further."

"I also can go no further," Pablo told him.

Aguila sighed. He could not blame these men. It was a risky
mission they were upon, with no assurance they would complete it alive. The region itself was a killer. Bands of Comanche and Kiowa crossed these plains at all points, at all times.
They would indeed be lucky if they did not run into one of
those bands even in this empty expanse of the world.

"Who else wishes to return to de Bexar?" Aguila asked.

Three others hung their heads and said they would also return to San Antonio. These five men had decided to desert
their mission. The conflict of their decision to leave their
friends in such hostile country could be seen in their eyes.
They started to beg Aguila to forgive them. He cut them off,
knowing that these men were truly brave beyond and above
all others.

"Peace, my friends. I know that you are all brave men, truly
I do. And that you are my personal friends. But you have
families who depend upon you. Go home with my thanks and
the thanks and gratitude, I'm sure, of Senor and Senora Rodriguez."

He turned to the men who had said nothing. "And you,
Senor du Bois? And you, José and Eduardo?"

A grin flashed across the Frenchman's face. Like Milton, he
used the sharp blade of his knife every morning to keep his
face clean-shaven. A small, polished silver hand mirror aided
him in keeping his thin line of a mustache neatly trimmed. "I
have no family waiting for me in San Antonio, amigo. Many
wives, but they have other men they call husband." Jean du
Bois laughed happily. "No, amigo, I will stay with you and
our big friend, Senor Milton Hicks. I think that if you follow
that man long enough, he will lead you into one hell of a
fight."

Aguila returned his grin.

"We will follow where you lead, *patrón*," José Sanchez said, speaking for himself and Eduardo Gutierrez. Only completion of their mission, their death, or orders from Aguila himself would turn these men aside from their duty.

Aguila did not ask Pancho what he would do. To have done so would be an insult to the heavy man. Pancho had turned his horse to join Milton before the conversation had even ended. He could never return to his wife and children and say that he had deserted his adopted son on the edge of the dreaded Llano Estacado in the middle of Comanche country. He would have to leave home.

"Aguila, my friend, you ride on, and we will take care of our dead," Juan told him. He looked at the broad back of Milton, who sat his horse, ready to follow the Indians when the final decision was made. "I do not like that man because he is an arrogant Yanqui. And because I know inside, deep down in my heart and soul, that I fear this half-savage man. But I also know, amigo, that if anyone can rescue the little Josephine, it is that big man."

All of the men agreed with him.

Aguila raised his hand in farewell, and he and his small band started on a journey that would carry them deeper into the private playground of the fierce Comanche.

Chapter Sixteen

The Comanche raiders did not turn west into the Llano Estacado but continued north along its edge. In this direction they would reach the Río Colorado and camp for the night. They should reach the river well before dark.

They were now in the tall grass area just on the outer rim of the Llano. The land was rolling, with large washes that made riding harder. Tall trees could be seen on the banks of small streams that held only a trickle of water at this time of the year. Many of the trees were at the bottom of the dried washes themselves, sucking what little moisture there was from underground sources with their long taproots.

Milton had hoped that the Indians would change direction and move directly into the Llano. If they had turned two hours earlier he would have known where they were going and would have had a chance to get ahead of them. Maybe he could do a little ambushing himself and start picking off the Comanche braves one at a time. His actions would not make the red men give up their captive, but he could sure whittle down the odds a little.

If the band turned then, they would have to stop at the secret water holes known to him. Milton was one of the very few outside of the Comanche and Kiowa tribes who knew the location of some of these water holes. Five years earlier, while hunting a stray horse, Milton had come upon an old Comanche who had been trampled by an angry buffalo. While taking the old man deep into the Llano Estacado where his camp was located, the Comanche had shown Milton the location of some of the water holes. He begged Milton never to let anyone know where he got his information.

The Comanche people were so unpredictable that the old man had asked Milton to let him go into camp alone when they reached their destination. He feared he might not be able to save the life of the man who had befriended him. Milton had turned his horse and ridden two days and nights without pause to get out of the immediate home territory of the Comanche. He never knew whether any of the old man's band had tried to follow him.

He had also found some of the water holes himself while on expeditions in the Llano. He had a knack for finding water, which was strange for a mountain-raised man.

Midafternoon brought Milton to a slight rise of land. A small saddle separated the two rises. The trail he was following led through the saddle. Under normal circumstances a slight change in topography would have made little difference. There were no large clumps of brush or outcropping of rock to hide anyone. But when chasing a people who could hide behind a blade of grass, long, low ridges were dangerous. This terrain could hide half the Comanche nation.

Milton signaled that they were coming to a dangerous area and the men would be wise to be especially watchful. He cocked his rifle and loosened the war ax in his belt. He kicked his horse forward and rode through the low saddle. The Indians were not in sight, but they could be in shallow holes in the grass. Another fold of land lay in front of him. The band of red men were already across the second rise of land and hidden from view. He wanted to see them and get their count. The Comanche could not be seen, but the gut-tight feeling of Milton's sixth sense played its tune of warning. He had a feeling that some of the band was missing from the count.

He rode slowly down the slight rise and through the shallow valley. The heat was stifling, and it was still and quiet. Not a blade of grass moved. No pheasants or quail flew from cover at his approach. Not a sight or sound of the swift, long-legged rabbit of the prairie was to be seen or heard. Only the

heat, silence, and buffalo grass seemed present. But the tall
American sensed a fourth unseen thing: an enemy lying in
ambush. The wide-brimmed hat shaded his darting eyes from
the direct glare of the bright sun.

Milton reached the top of the second rise as the search party
rode into the shallow valley behind him. He stopped and
waited. This would be it.

Three Indians sprang from hidden holes to the rear of the
search party and gave out savage war cries that shattered the
silence of the afternoon heat. They stood brandishing their
bows and arrows at the white men, but held their fire.

While the three men with the bows and arrows drew the
attention of the white men, two other Comanche braves
stepped out of holes to the left. They dropped to their knees
and fired as one.

A round lead ball hit Aguila just above the knee and passed
through his leg and deep into the chest of his horse. Both man
and beast fell to the ground in a cloud of dust. The Mexican's
right leg was caught under the thrashing horse, pinning him
to the ground. Pancho was the first man off his horse. He ran
to Aguila and knelt at his young friend's side, ignoring the
Indians who were shooting at him. The heavy-bodied Mexican
took hold of the saddle with both of his powerful hands and
used brute strength to lift the dying animal from the ground.
Aguila pulled his leg free.

The second rifle bullet struck Jean du Bois low in his left
shoulder, knocking him from his horse. He landed flat on his
back in the hot sand and lay staring up at the bright sun in
stunned amazement.

José and Eduardo jumped from their horses and started returning the rifle fire.

The Indians knew that they were too far from Milton for
him to have effective rifle fire. During the initial encounter,
they did not have to worry about him.

Milton whirled his pony around and, using his feet, dug his
toes into the shoulders of the little mount. This was a signal

for the horse to stand still. The Indians should have worried about Milton, for he was one of the best rifle shots in northern Mexico. At the same instant the horse stopped in its turn, Milton brought his long rifle to his shoulder, took a quick look to judge the distance of the three Indians closest to him, and fired the instant a target came into sight. For the normal rifleman using a normal charge of powder, the ball would not have reached the target, let alone have been accurate. When Milton rode into the plains country where there was unlimited view for long distances, he carried an extra charge of powder in his rifle. He had surprised more than one enemy with the long-range accuracy of the extra-heavy-duty Pennsylvania-made "Kentucky" rifle. He was also one of those rare marksmen who could judge distance, windage, and lead time in the split second it took to sight his rifle. Every shot was straight and true, and reached its target, unless the target made an erratic move while the bullet was in the air.

Milton dug his heels into the sides of the pony before the Indian dropped to the ground. He poured powder into the rifle, dropped wadding and lead ball down the barrel, struck the rifle butt on the ground to set the ball and charge, raised and cocked the hammer, dropped a cap into the firing hole, took aim, and killed a second Comanche brave. All of this was done while his horse was in a dead run. Now there was only one more Comanche left with bow and arrows.

The two Indians with the rifles broke and ran. Above all else, the rifles must be saved.

The third Indian with bow and arrows stood his ground, firing three arrows before Milton could close with him. Milton swung the heavy rifle like a club, and the barrel split the Comanche's skull wide open. The brave joined his brothers to hunt buffalo and antelope in the celestial hunting ground beyond the sun.

Milton's horse staggered and faltered. The man pulled back on the reins and stepped from the saddle. He knelt and fired in one fluid motion. The fourth Comanche brave fell, and the fifth paused long enough to pick up the second rifle.

The tall man turned and saw that his horse was still standing, but it was quivering violently. An arrow was embedded
up to the feathers in the war pony's chest. Milton pulled off
the saddle and bridle, dropping them to the ground. He then
pulled his pistol and said a short prayer in Cherokee, for at
times like these he was more comfortable with that language:
"Please forgive me, little brother horse, for taking your life,
but I do not wish to see you suffer." He shot the pony behind
the left ear. Milton looked down at the small horse that had
given him such good service these past three years. They had
traveled many miles together. He was not a sentimental man,
but he respected strength, intelligence, courage and loyalty,
even if they came from an animal.

He turned and walked over to each Indian he had killed. He
would go to each man and turn him over to peer intently into
his face for a short moment. Milton did not take scalps the way
some red men and white men did. Yet this was not because it
seemed barbarous to him; it was just a messy job he didn't
have time for. It did seem that he must look into the face of
every man he killed, just in case he ever saw that man in the
afterworld, or heaven, or Sky Rock, or wherever the spirit of a
man goes after life in this world.

Milton walked back to join the other men, carrying his saddle over his shoulder. These men could take the scalps back to
San Antonio as the other white men had done. There they
could tell the other white men how they would deal with the
red savages who invaded their homes. He looked around and
saw the two wounded men and the dead horse. They were
now six men with four horses. Not a good situation for white
men in the homeland of the Comanche, especially with two of
them wounded.

"It looks like it is the end of the chase, amigo," Aguila said
with a smile that was twisted with pain.

"I go on," Milton informed him.

Aguila was not surprised. In all truth, neither were the others. This man did things that seemed strange to others, but

they were normal to him. Yet Aguila felt he must ask, "By yourself? Alone?"

"With a horse, if possible. You take the other three horses. The other men who are not wounded can take turns riding one horse. When you get to the Río Concho you should find a small stand of trees to make a travois for the wounded. I will follow the Comanche."

There was a tone of finality in his voice that discouraged argument. He was to continue the chase, and nothing short of death would stop him. His friends had expected just that, yet they knew if anyone would return from the dead, it would be Milton Hicks.

"Pancho, your horse for our *compadre*," Aguila told his old friend.

Compadre is never used lightly by a Mexican. The term is used between the father of a son and his godfather, or between the closest of friends who are all but brothers in blood.

Without a word, Pancho stripped his saddle from the back of the big gray. He then put the long-legged man's saddle on the back of his favorite horse. With a gentle pat on the horse's shoulder he whispered into the animal's ear: "You be a good *caballo* for the Don Milton. Do not make me ashamed of you. Take him fast and sure across the dreaded Llano Estacado. He is the only one who can save the Senorita Josephine."

Pancho would have kissed his big horse on the nose if so many had not been present. He was sure he had seen the big gray for the last time. The Mexican handed the reins to Milton.

Milton walked over to where Jean du Bois lay.

"Milton. Milton, come close," Jean called in a weak voice.

Milton knelt down to hear the Frenchman.

"My real name is Paseur. Jean Perrault Paseur. My father was a major in the Personal Guard for the Emperor Napoleon. My family came with others to Alabama in America in 1815," Jean told Milton. "If you find my bones someday, it will be those of Jean Paseur. I want someone to know what happened to me."

"I will tell the priest," Milton promised his friend. Then he said, "It is Jean Paseur if you die. It is Jean du Bois if we meet in a cantina in de Bexar."

Jean smiled weakly.

Milton stepped up to the back of the big gray and sat looking down at his friends. He did not offer to shake hands with the men. With a short, curt nod as his only good-bye, he rode off, pointing the horse due north.

"*Viaje con don Dios, mi amigo.* Travel with god, my friend," Aguila called after Milton.

"*Hasta luego*, Don Milton. May the Blessed Virgin and Mother of the True God go with you." Pancho whispered a prayer and crossed himself.

José and Eduardo crossed themselves. "When we get back to the ranch I will light a candle for this man," José said.

He stood watching Milton ride off. "No! I will light one hundred candles for this man!"

"Have you ever seen such shooting in all your life? To shoot like that I would become the new president of Mexico," Eduardo said in admiration.

"Mexico needs a new president," Aguila told the men.

The two vaqueros did not comment. They were only peons and did not think of politics or anything outside the world of their ranch life.

"There goes *un mucho hombre*, Aguila," Jean whispered loudly, his dry throat rasping out the words.

"Sí. He is truly a man of *huevos grandes*. Those the size of a huge stud," Aguila agreed. "But maybe this time, though, he finds big trouble. More than even Milton Hicks can handle."

Jean gave a grin over the pain of his wound. "I bet you the best bottle of wine in all of Mexico we will see him in San Antonio again."

"Ha! With this man I do not bet against," Aguila said. He looked after his big Yanqui friend. "When Don Milton returns with the young Josephine I will buy wine for everyone. And the best bottle of wine in all Mexico will go to our great and brave friend, Milton Hicks."

"He may even return with my fine big gray," said Pancho hopefully.

Chapter Seventeen

Milton rode over the rise and found the tracks of the raiding party. The Indians were already out of sight. He did not urge his horse to a faster pace. He knew that he and the animal would need all their strength before this chase was finished. The Comanche might take their captive into the northern plains to trade her with another band of Comanche or Kiowa. Either way, he was in for a long haul.

Extra care would have to be taken from here on out. Four more braves of the raiding party were now dead. The band of Comanche were being pressed so hard by the white men that they had to leave their dead upon the field. That was something no Comanche wanted to do. In fact, most Indians did not wish to leave their dead without administering the last rites of a warrior. And now one lone white man had the audacity to follow them deep into their own domain. They could not allow him to leave the Llano Estacado if he penetrated it, and it was better still to kill him before they turned into the rugged plains. He had to be killed as an example to the nearest white settlement. His blood must cool their hate and anger, and his dead soul ease the angered spirits of their dead.

Milton had been following them for three hours when a rifle ball came from out of hiding and hit the horse he was riding in the right eye. The big horse seemed to lose all the strength throughout its huge frame all at once; it fell apart and crumpled in its tracks.

As the horse fell, Milton jumped free just as the second rifle ball cracked harmlessly over his head. This band had some excellent marksmen. He was glad they had only two rifles.

Milton was also ashamed that he had been ambushed. His mind was not on his business and he missed seeing this potential danger spot.

Each rifleman fired one shot apiece, then quickly retreated on foot. This tall man and his quick reaction and accurate shooting were beginning to be both respected and feared. It was seldom that any one man, be he red or white, was good enough to kill five Comanche braves in such a short time. The Kwaharies would have to face much laughter and criticism from the other bands in the tribe. The overbearing Yamparikas, the Rooteaters, were going to be the worst of all.

Milton pulled the saddle off the dead mount and carried it to be hidden in the lone clump of tumbleweed. He kept the water canteens and tucked the venison jerky that was wrapped in doeskin inside his buckskin shirt. The doeskin bag that held the silver goblet was taken out of the saddle bags and slung around his neck. The money was left in the saddle bags. He would need none where he was going. When he was ready to leave he took a close look around him, permanently recording the area in his mind. He would remember this place for years.

Without another look at the dead horse, he started off in a ground-eating dogtrot. He had not even thought about the direction he would take. The evening sun was to his left, and when night came he would be facing the North Star.

He ran hour after hour, on and on. He did not stop to eat or drink, but put a piece of jerky in his mouth to chew on as he ran. The red man had run on foot for thousands of years before the white man brought the horse to this continent. Most red men could run more than fifty miles a day, day after day, then fight a battle at the end of the run. Most Indians could run great distances when called upon even after the coming of the horse. Milton was one of those. He had been a swift, long-distance runner in his youth. He had been one of the best message runners as a young man, running from village to village. His running had been in the mountains rather than the flat plains he was now in. The Cherokee still used their legs in their natural habitat and were not as dependent on the horse

as the Plains Indians and the white man. Milton's ability had
not failed him over the years. Hard, long running hurt him
more now than when he was younger, but his mature strength
and the endurance of a man in excellent physical condition
and the prime of his life were his biggest advantages. He
would chase this Kwaharie band of Comanche all the way to
Canada or to the interior of Mexico if need be. Whichever
direction they took, that would be his direction.

The first hour of the run had been his worst. His muscles,
long asleep, began to scream in agony at their rude awakening.
His lungs had shrunk over the past few idle months, and they
also screamed at the expanding effort placed upon them by his
extra-deep gulps of hot, dry air. He began to catch his second
wind, and his entire body settled into one dull ache.

He set his mind on what his teacher had taught him; "to set
the pace of a warrior." The simple explanation was to let mind
take over matter. Not many learned to set the pace of a warrior. Milton had. He learned all that his Cherokee teachers had
taught him. His most interesting lessons had come from those
the white men called "medicine men." There was more than
one order of medicine man. The old man who had taught him
to set the pace of a warrior was called an *anelisgi*, "those who
think purposefully." The one who came closest to what the
white's called a medicine man was a *didahanowesgi*, "curer of
them, he." The most powerful of the medicine men, perhaps
the tribe, were the men who took care of the spiritual and
religious needs of the people. It was they who tended the eternal *atsila galukawetiyu*, "sacred fire" of the Cherokee in the
sheona, "Town House." These men were called *adawehi*, for
which there was no real English translation. The men most
feared were the imprecator called an *uta igaweski*, "evil,
speaker of it, he." Those men of mystery, or things that "go
bump in the night," were called *sunayi anedai*, "they walk
about at night." One of his grandfathers had been an *anelisgi*,
"those who think purposefully," and was also called *udanoti*,
"a man of soul or feeling." These town philosophers were the

thinkers and intellectuals. The man he most respected was his grandfather who was an *adawehi*. He had power.

Milton breathed deeply at regular intervals and let his body and mind become one, then become suspended in limbo through psychological command. His mind began to float into a peaceful remembrance of his youth, when things were simple and good. He recalled pleasant things—like the older girl who had taught him one spring day beside a bubbling mountain stream the difference between a young boy's thinking about taking a woman and the actual experience of doing so. Cherokee women were not the wanton hussies the white women called them, but they were more responsive to their men than their puritanical white sisters. To them nature was a gift of the Creative Being and any gift he gave could not be bad and evil. There were no bastard children among the Cherokee. If a man could not take a child, any child, to raise as his own, he was not a true Cherokee. The greatness of fatherhood was not the conception but the bringing up of a young man to be a warrior or a girl to be a good woman. An idiot could perform the act of conception.

When a man set the pace of a warrior, he did not remove himself from the real world. Every sense in him was honed to razor-edge sharpness. He could detect the slightest movement with extra-sensitive eyes and hear with extra sensitive ears. His body could even distinguish the different rises and falls of temperature as he ran up and down the slight rises of the ground. It seemed that his whole body had become a large barometer of the entire physical world. He felt the desire to pull off his clothes, as his fathers of old had done, so he could take accurate measurements of all the elements around him. But along with that feeling of drifting gaiety were the senses that controlled a man in everyday life. One of those was his ability to reason. To run and act with purpose was what it was all about—to be ever in command of all his faculties.

Shortly after dark the soft glow of the Indians' fire told Milton that he had caught up with the band. He chose the best area to defend if necessary and built a small fire out of buffalo chips. The fire was not built out of necessity but to let the Indians know that he was still with them. It would give them something to think about.

He watched the enemy's fire for a while, then moved away from his own campfire to sleep. Milton was sure the Comanche would not try to take his camp the first night. But men of the frontier lived because they tried to figure all options before they acted. And after what would happen tomorrow morning, he would not have many peaceful nights from here on out.

The Comanche saw his fire. Some of the young braves wanted to pay this tall man a visit, even at the risk of losing their spirits to the night. It seemed unreasonable for a white man to be as determined and relentless as a Comanche. This one had to be gotten rid of, and all the other white men such as he, before they became too many and ran the red man from the land of the buffalo and antelope. The buffalo and antelope were placed on the plains of the red man by the Great Spirit for his food and shelter, and they were not for the white man. If they killed enough white men, maybe they would leave Comanche land alone.

These Plains Indians felt the white man should stay back in the tree line in the east and to the south of the mountain range in their southern region in the east. They had heard many stories from the Indians in the east who had been overrun and destroyed by the white men with hair on their faces and with a strange language. They were new kinds of Mexicans called Yanquis. It was from that area, from the southeast, that they felt their most dangerous threat. But those white devils were too far away to worry about. They had been told by the eastern and northern tribes that the white men were sending their medicine men among them to teach them a new religion. If the Indians did not accept this new religion, they were killed or driven off their land.

The Mexicans would steal their children to be slaves on their large cattle ranches and farms, but they were not interested in killing off all of the Indians. This land was of no value to them. But it was learned that these new Mexicans called

Yanquis believed God had given them all land to control and no others could hold it. These new white men did not believe the red men were real people. The Comanche knew this to be false, for were they not called "The People?"

But out here in this hostile country called the Great Plains, the Comanche was safe from those white men from the east. Even if those white men came, they would have no use for it, so why worry about such a stupid thing.

The chief of the raiding party held his young braves and would not let them go out after this unknown man. He had watched this tall man closely since he had first seen the search party following them. This one was not like the rest of the white men who had come to chase the Comanche. The tall one could read sign as well as his best trackers, and he knew every suitable place for an ambush by sight. It was only by luck that his riflemen had scored a hit this afternoon. The chief had never lost so many men in a raiding party. In fact, he had seldom lost this many men in a war party. Now, two encounters with this white man and he had lost five men. They had killed his horse, so now he ran after them on foot. This man ran hour after hour like the Comanche of old before the coming of the horse.

He watched the white man's fire, and he knew deep inside his savage warrior's heart that this man was a great warrior. For the first time in his life the chief was concerned. This man would not give up his chase until he was dead or the white girl had been returned to her people. They were eleven against one, but the chief had a feeling that they were not enough for this cunning warrior who followed them. This was a bad thought for a Comanche to have. If he had more rifles, this man who ran like the Kwaharie of old could be stopped. The chief·shook himself. He was ashamed. He had been fighting white men all his life, and here he was thinking like a young boy who had not yet become a warrior.

An older man walked up beside the chief. He was getting too old to go on raiding parties, but the men liked to have him along. It was not only because he had been a great warrior of much fame in his younger days, but because he was also a great *puhakut* who could talk to the spirits. Because of his knowledge of the songs and dances that pleased the buffalo spirits, this old *puhakut* never failed to call the buffalo down from the north every winter. More and more were coming every year at his call. The buffalo meant everything to the Comanche. The big animals provided their people with food, hides to make shelters, clothes, robes for warmth from the bitter winter winds of the plains and to cover their war shields; they provided bone and sinew for the bow. Even the waste of the big beast provided the Comanche with fuel for fire in this treeless homeland of theirs. A man who could call down the buffalo every year must truly be close to the Great Spirit.

"This one may have a bad spirit in his liver," the old *puhakut* told Run-to-water, breaking into the thoughts of the chief. "If the spirit in his liver is strong, then we cannot kill him. I do not have the proper things with me to make his evil spirit weak so we can kill him."

"Hump!" grunted Run-to-water.

Rolling Bush, the old *puhakut*, looked at the younger man beside him in the dark. "His spirit is very evil. I can feel it."

The old man had relieved himself of responsibility by telling the chief that he did not have the proper equipment to ward off this man's evil. Now whatever happened was out of his power and control.

Run-to-water did not look at the older man, but kept his eyes on the distant fire that was being allowed to die out. "He does not have a bad spirit, old one. He is just a good warrior."

The old man smiled to himself in the dark. This man they had chosen as chief was a smart man. Run-to-water would have made a good *puhakut* if Rolling Bush could have influenced him to take that path when he was a young man. But he could not influence him to do so. So much the loss for the fraternity of spirit callers.

"Do you remember the white man who brought Missing-two-toes back to camp five years ago?" he asked the chief.

"This is that same man. I have talked many times with Missing-two-toes about this man. He is not from this land, but
many miles to the east in another country. To the east toward
the rising sun, where the Mexican people are called Yanquis.
Missing-two-toes does not know if he is from a tribe from
across the water where the white man came from, or who he
is. Missing-two-toes did not ask. But he says this tall man can
speak the language of the Comanche and the Mexican. He also
speaks one that is foreign to us. He is a mighty warrior. He
will not be so easy to kill, this one."

Run-to-water gave another grunt and walked off to make
sure the girl had been fed. The chief would not stop the old
man from telling the younger braves that the tall man had an
evil spirit. Like most leaders, he had learned long ago to plan
for all contingencies and that there was always room for com-
promise. These rumors and thinking that the tall man may
have a bad spirit might be an honorable way to return the girl
to the white man if they could not kill him. Maybe he really
did have an evil spirit that would keep them from killing him.
Run-to-water did not know of these things. Who was he, or
any man, to question the way the Great Spirit operated?

The chief had wanted to continue north to where the
Yamparika band roamed. He owed them a favor and wanted to
give them the girl. But he changed his mind and would turn
directly into the Llano Estacado. He would repay that favor in
another manner and not with the girl. If they held out against
this mad man for four or five days, they would be near the
main village and be too many even for Tall One.

He looked down at the young girl in the firelight. She was
pretty of feature as far as white women went. She was a little
on the skinny side, and not of very good physical stamina. If
she had not been riding a mule, she could not have kept up
with the band. Any Comanche woman could do this thing if
there were no horses, and carry a load on her back. If a child
must be born, then she would stop by the side of the trail and
catch up after giving birth.

Run-to-water was not interested in the girl. He had two

women who were sisters and made fine wives. He was glad to have the girl because he was always glad to capture a young one from the Mexicans. The Mexicans had been stealing Indians and making slaves of them ever since it could be remembered. He had lost two young brothers and a sister to the Mexicans many years ago. Now that he was a chief, he was able to command enough men to attack the white men. Most of the people he had captured were better than this girl. She was too weak and white to stand much physical punishment. If she survived, she would become strong and a wife to some brave. The women would see that she learned to be a good wife. If she died . . . Only the strong survived in Comanche land.

He glanced back to where the fire of Tall One had been. All was now dark, and no one except the Great Spirit above knew where that big devil was hiding. One thing was certain. He was watching every move the camp made. A cold hand brushed his neck and shoulders. He shook himself. He was again ashamed, for no man had ever affected him like this before.

Run-to-water decided he would place the horses and the girl in the center of the camp. Half of the men would be awake and on guard all night. They would protest, but he would demand it. And they could do without the services of the girl for one night, or maybe until they got back to camp.

Milton was indeed watching the camp at that very moment. He had left the fire long before it went out and crossed the lower branch of the Río Colorado. It was a narrow stream that he could step across at this point, but there was enough water to fill his empty canteen. It took a lot of water to keep a man running in this heat. But now that the sun had set, and at this altitude, it would not be hot much longer. He was in for a cold, uncomfortable night.

He found a place to hide well out of the possible range of a night guard. The fires had died down, and he could no longer make out human forms. It would be a moonless night, and he would not be able to get off a shot until someone lit a fire just before dawn. Then after the shot, he would move quickly under the cover of darkness.

He smiled in anticipation of the coming of the dawn.

Chapter Eighteen

The coldest part of the day anywhere in the world is just before dawn. It is no different on the Llano Estacado in West Texas, even in the early part of summer.

Milton chose this time, just before dawn, to move closer to the Comanche camp. He would move to a point he had chosen beforehand. There he would wait his first chance at a kill. He knew the chief would hold his braves in and not let them wander around in the dark looking for him. But if he gave them enough trouble they would start getting jumpy, and jumpy men make mistakes.

A piece of metal struck a piece of flint and sparked brightly. The small spark fell on some kindling and dried grass and began to grow in size and brightness as someone blew on the spark. Milton raised his rifle and took aim on the outline of the head that was beginning to appear. A moment later and the features of the person bent over the glowing coal took form. It was the young girl, Josephine. Milton relaxed his grip on the trigger but did not lower the rifle from his shoulder.

Slightly to the left of Josephine a second spark was struck. Milton waited only for the outline of the head to appear this time. Before it was completed he squeezed the trigger.

The heavy round ball struck the brave just below the left eye. The impact of the bullet shattered the cheekbone and drove the splintered bone ahead of the ball into the brain. Brain, blood, and skull bone splattered a young brave lying nearby. The left eye of the wounded brave popped out of its socket and rolled sightlessly on the sandy floor of the West

Texas prairie. The optic nerve, still connected to his empty socket, kept the eye from rolling off in the dark.

Before the kneeling man hit the ground, Milton moved under the cover of darkness and noise. Both fires were scattered, and the girl's wrists and ankles were quickly bound together.

Bullets from the two rifles and arrows from the bowmen bounced off the rocks Milton had just left. He crawled back to his hiding place and put a piece of leathery jerky into his mouth to stay his hunger. While he watched and listened to the confusion going on at the Indian camp across the river, he hung the pouch containing the silver goblet and water canteens around his neck. Then he checked the rest of his equipment and was ready to move out.

The chief called orders to his men. The horses and mules were to be gathered and they would ride immediately. They would ride west and deep into the Llano Estacado to their village. They would be on their way now, quickly! If anyone wanted meat, he would eat it raw.

The subchief led out, leading Josephine's mule. They were followed by two braves leading the captured animals. The remaining men spread out as a rear guard to protect the last of the caravan from attack. After a short distance the chief pulled up his mount and turned to face their old camp.

The old *puhakut* pulled up alongside the chief. "We cannot kill Tall One," Rolling Bush told Run-to-water. "His evil spirit will protect him."

The chief only grunted and turned his horse to follow his men. He knew that spirits were free to come and go as they wished. An evil spirit was as strong as a good spirit and could not be affected by a mere man. That was why they had to have a *puhakut*. The *puhakut* had learned all the ways to deal with these spirits. These ceremonies and rituals had been handed down from generation to generation; each ceremony and ritual was different in order to placate a different spirit.

But this man following them, what about him? He was not an evil spirit, no matter what the old man said. He was just a good warrior with a good rifle. More of his men would be dead before this day was over. He would not be able to stop his young men from trying to ambush Tall One. It would be a great honor to the one who killed this great warrior. The young men would have to try, and he could not stop them. They were Comanche, "The People," and not like other men. A Comanche was a supreme individualist. A Comanche was not bashful when it came to breaking a law he thought was wrong, even if it meant his own death.

Milton watched the outline of the men against the horizon as they rode off. He could easily kill another man now, but he would give away his position and it was getting light. He noticed that the Indians' direction of travel had changed, taking them into the Llano Estacado. Now he would have to suffer the heat of this barren land the Mexicans also called Comancheria. Things had to break soon, or the raiding party would have the protection of their entire band. It would then be nearly impossible to rescue Josephine. It would be just as bad if they ran upon another band of hunters or raiders. He could not trade for her. Not only had he killed six Comanche warriors, but the Comanche would not want to trade her life for his when they could have both. Why had they not already taken his life? One massed rush would do it.

An hour after sunrise the sun had burnt off the coolness of the night and evaporated the dew. It seemed that they journeyed into an area that had a stomachache and in its fits of sickness had spewed up rocks and dug out deep, long canyons. These "bad lands" were on the eastern rim of the true Llano Estacado, the high plains being elevated above the rough lands. From a distance the rim of the high plains looked as if it were capped by rock. Reaching the Llano would be a rough climb on both man and horses.

After reaching the flat plains it seemed to Milton that the heat increased. Traveling through this sea of grass during the heat of summer, a man would never believe snowstorms, driven by howling winds straight from the north pole, covered these plains during winter months. Not after days such as this one. There was no wind, not a cloud in the clear, empty sky to carry a drop of moisture. The searing heat from the hot sun made the cool of the predawn seem a lie.

As the sun rose higher and began to cast down its heat, the Comanche began to hold their rawhide sunshades above their heads. They normally carried these squared sunshades on their backs when they were not in use. Because of this custom, some called the Comanche Kwahihekena, "Sunshades on Their Backs." In the sign language of the plains, the Comanche were known as the Snakes. The sign was made by placing the right hand palm downward, with the forearm across the front of the body, and moving it to the right with a wiggling motion.

Milton never slowed his pace, keeping two to three miles behind the Comanche now that he was in open terrain. He never bothered to pause for a drink, but drank sparingly as he ran. After the first thirty minutes he had caught his second wind, and he now felt he could run forever. The run the afternoon before had been a hard one for him. His muscles, tight from the idle winter, were now beginning to stretch and become pliable.

He looked at the prairie around him. Although he had seen it before, it never ceased to amaze him that the land was so flat. It was so flat for miles and miles in each direction that it seemed he was in the center of a plate, its outer rims slowly rising to form the horizon. He was in a sea of grass. A sailor would feel right at home on the Llano Estacado once he became accustomed to the color, for he could use sea navigation just as well on the plains as at sea.

Off to his right Milton saw a buffalo and two calves. The calves were latecomers and had missed the migration of the herd as it went north. How far were they from where he ran? He could not tell for certain. He was not used to the flat land of the prairie and could not accurately judge the distance.

How many days did he have before they reached the main camp? Three? Four? There was no indication from the pace the chief had set. It had been steady from the start. There had been no increase to indicate that they had changed direction and were now on their way to family and home. Huh! He had better stop thinking like a white man. It would get him killed. These men were warriors and spent much of their time away from home hunting and raiding to feed their families. They did not, like white men, increase their speed because they were being followed by enemies. A Comanche would not knowingly lead an enemy of strength near the camp of his women and children.

There was not much change in the landscape of this monotonous sea of grass, but Milton saw all of the slight changes that could be used as ambush sites. He was extra alert to these areas. He was now alone, and Josephine's only hope. He did not fear death itself, but he did not wish to go to the afterworld beyond the sun so young in life. If the girl was going to be taken back to her family, he must stay alive for both of them.

Run-to-water called a rest halt. He rode to the rear of his little caravan and sat his horse, looking out over the vast, open prairie. It looked empty and deserted except for one lone figure that came toward him at a slow trot. The white man came in a steady, dogged pace that could eventually run down a horse. This was the pace that was used to run deer, buffalo, antelope, and other animals into the ground before the horse. The swift-footed antelope of the plains would succumb to such a relentless, driving chase. In the end, it would stand on trembling legs, weak and exhausted from lack of water, food, and rest. The animal would stand docile, waiting for the man to do with it what he would. His grandfather had told stories of such men as this. There were not many left who could run down an antelope. This one following them was one of those few.

"This man has an evil spirit in his liver. We cannot kill him," the old man repeated, jarring Run-to-water back to the present. "If we give him the girl, he will leave us. If we do not, more men will die. His evil spirit will protect him."

"It is a man's destiny in life to die. How he does that is up to the Great One," the chief told him. "He is just a good warrior, old man. Just a good warrior."

"No man should say that the Great One always decides," Rolling Bush said. "That is why he gave man a brain and good luck. We are now having bad luck with this one following us. We must do something, or he will affect all of the men. He has an evil spirit."

"He is just a good warrior," the chief repeated. "We will talk of it no more."

Josephine sat her mount, her head still bowed. She was a picture of subdued dejection. Her spirits had risen when the rifle shot had killed one of her captors earlier that morning. But she had been rebound and placed on her mule to ride some more. When the sun came up she saw that the same man on foot was still following. He was indeed a brave man, but what could one man do against so many? It was hopeless.

This once fiery-tempered, spoiled young lady was now a woman who would never again take life or other people's subjugation to her every whim for granted. But she was not broken. Her steel had been retempered and she had been molded into a stronger woman. She had been molded into the type of woman it took to settle, endure, and civilize the rough frontier of Texas. Now that she knew who she was and what she had to offer the world, she had to escape. She didn't want to spend her life mothering half-breed children, most of whom would die before they reached their first birthday. She did not want to live in camp after camp, following the buffalo.

She looked back at the lone figure following them on foot. He was her only hope. A very slim, if not impossible, hope. But she needed something to hold on to.

Milton took one short pause to drink some water. Then he moved on to follow the Kwaharie, who had begun to move again. The red men had developed a new tactic to keep the white man off balance. A rider would jump from his horse to the back of another horse ridden by another rider. From the great distance it would look as if there was only one rider on the horse and appear that one of the horses was riderless.

When the tall one looked up he would see what appeared to be one man missing. This could mean that one of the men was on a possible ambush mission. Some of the young braves probably felt that their spirit was as strong as his.

This procedure did keep him off balance. He had to stop and check places that he would otherwise pass and leave unnoticed. Or he ran in wide zigzag angles to keep from running directly behind the Comanche. He had to stop or slow down to check hoof tracks to see if their impression indicated one or two riders on a horse. This was not always an accurate way to tell, but he had to check. This made him run farther and harder just to keep up. But a little thing like that would not bother him. His entire being was set on one object, and he intended to possess that object.

Chapter Nineteen

The shot rang out to Milton's right. He was facedown on the ground before the bullet or sound reached him. As soon as he saw the puff of smoke from the rifle, he hit the ground. He did not fall like many men, making sure they landed in a good spot or not on their equipment. When he was being shot at, he relaxed and fell as if he had been shot, landing where he fell and not worrying about it. The Comanche were well out of effective range, and the ball landed to his right front.

Milton lay a moment, then raised himself to his knees and quickly fell again. There was no shot from the second rifleman. His few moments upright gave him a chance to see three braves running to join their friends. One carried a rifle and the other two bows and arrows. They did not want to lose either of the rifles and always sent along plenty of help. The mission of the extra braves was not to get their friends back to safety, but the rifles.

The three braves had gotten well out of rifle range even for Milton's long rifle by the time he got to his feet. There was danger of the second rifleman lying in wait to gun him down as he continued forward, but he did not think this was a real threat. He knew he was safe after ten or fifteen steps and he could count the riders.

Two frightened doe and three fawn ran between him and the Comanche. If he had the time he would have liked to kill one for fresh meat. Instead, he placed another piece of leathery jerked venison into his mouth. He would also conserve his water, for he knew of none for the next two days.

Milton ran easily, ignoring the heat and discomfort of his

steaming buckskins. It was on this run that he had made his only mistake. He wished now that he had taken off his leather shirt and exchanged it for a cotton one. He knew that he could not run under this hot sun without a shirt. The dust didn't bother him. It was another windless day, and the dust he kicked up never got much above his knees.

Run-to-water didn't halt at noon. He hadn't stopped because he was trying to outrun the tall white man following them. The Comanche chief knew that the man following them would not stop, even if they rode all night and all the next day. The only thing that would stop him from running was if his great heart broke. His men also could not be pushed too hard. If he tried, they would rebel. But he had to get as close to the main camp as possible and hope they ran into a party of their men. He could not send ahead to the camp for help. For what? To handle one man? If he did call for help, this would be the last party of any type he would lead as chief. He was in a dilemma.

He could not set a steady pace either. If a steady pace was set, Tall One could use the pattern of speed to get ahead of them and set up his own ambush. Run-to-water made sure he, too, varied his direction every once in a while, never going in a straight line. The band also had to stop at night, which would make it easier for Tall One to set up ambushes and kill more of his men. That morning before dawn Tall One had made them aware that he would fight at night as well as during the day. Run-to-water was angry at himself. A man could not return with honor after losing so many men, no matter how many captives and horses were brought back.

There would be much wailing of mothers and wives and daughters upon their return. Even in his own tepee there would be wailing and crying for a nephew. His sister had lost her husband, and now she lived in his tepee with her children. His nephew was one of the men who had been killed. He wished he could give his sister to Tall One as a wife. He would not only get a sister out of his house, but also gain a great warrior for his band.

He had to do something, but he didn't know what it would be. Many of the young men were already talking about the evil spirit that protected Tall One. That was the reason he had not been killed in the last ambush, or so they were beginning to believe. None of them took notice that the range had been too great for accurate shooting, or that Tall One had dropped to the ground for protection as any intelligent warrior would do. If a spirit protected him, he would not have dropped to the ground. He would not hesitate to walk into the camp and take what he wanted. Run-to-water would not order the men to attack him. If he did and they refused, he would lose too much face. The only ones who would tackle this tall man were those who felt their medicine was as strong as his.

All they could do was keep moving in a proper, warriorlike manner and try to get as near camp as possible. Suddenly Run-to-water changed his mind. No matter what was said, he would send a rider ahead for help tomorrow. He shuddered at the thought.

As he ran Milton was thinking about the tactics of the Comanche chief. He was sure they were trying to get as close to their main camp as possible before stopping for the night. He was also certain they would be close enough by the next night for a rider to ride to the main camp for help. And the chief was smart enough not to be in too much of a hurry. Hurried and excited men made greater mistakes, and the Comanche had made no real mistakes on this trip.

Milton knew the young braves would try to ambush him again. He understood, for he himself was a warrior. What other way could a warrior be? He must become a man of honor if he would stand in the presence of his peers. The role of a warrior is to fight and seek honor. Any other existence is dull and makes a slow, boring life for a man of war. Most warriors would say they would die a slow, painful death if there ever came a time of permanent peace.

The Comanche again began to use tactics to confuse him as to how many riders there were at any given time. He was sure they were getting ready to set up another ambush. He was also sure that this tactic was slowing him down. It was a good tactic, and one he would file away in his mental catalog of survival.

There was no warning puff of smoke to signal the second ambush. The bullet from the rifle struck the ground to his right front as before. The marksman needed to set some windage on his sighting, but that would come as he drew closer. The rifleman was too far away for accurate shooting.

Milton dropped to the ground in his usual manner. He was unlucky enough to fall into the private domain of the agony of Texas, a bed of red ants. His sudden fall upon their home and castle sent them angrily scurrying in all directions, dispatching runners with messages of alarm to the outer limits of their empire. He quickly rolled off the mound, hoping that he had moved fast and far enough.

He quickly rose to his knees and then fell facedown. A second rifle ball went singing its song of death in search of a listener. It would not find one on this trip. The man with the second rifle was an excellent marksman, Milton observed. He was also closer this time.

During his short stay upright, Milton saw the first rifleman and his two aides running away. That meant both rifles had been discharged and it was safe for him to stand. The distance was much too far for bow and arrow.

As he jumped to his feet, he felt a sting on the right side of his neck. A small warrior from the Formicidae family had found its adversary and attacked. Milton brushed the little insect from his neck, taking care not to kill or injure it. An animal attacked in defense or justice. A man would attack to kill and mangle for no other reason than pure, damned orneriness and meanness if he could find no other motive.

As he ran, he quickly judged the distance of the second rifleman and the two braves running alongside him. There was no doubt in his mind which of the three men he was going to shoot. He would get rid of the one with the rifle. The Indian was too good a marksman to let him run free with another chance to try again.

The distance was not too great for Milton and his long rifle with its overcharge of powder. He dropped to one knee, aimed high above the rifleman's head, and squeezed the trigger. The flash of the cap of fulminate of mercury ignited the gun powder, and another human life was snuffed out as quickly as the gun powder burnt itself out. One of the braves grabbed the rifle from his falling comrade without breaking stride. The rifle must be saved.

Milton poured powder from his powder horn and began to run in his ground-eating dogtrot. He dropped the wadding and lead ball down the barrel and drove home the ramrod. He stopped when he reached the dead Indian and looked at the man. It had been a long shot, and the impact of the rifle ball had to hit a vital spot to kill him. The ball had hit the man's spine just below his belt. Milton was proud of that shot.

He turned the man over and looked into his face. This man was not a Comanche but a Lipan. His eyebrows and eyelashes had been plucked, as was their custom, and that of the Comanche and Kiowa as well. But he had the markings of a Lipan. He was young, in his late teens or early twenties. Two scalp locks hung from his belt. Both were fresh and of black hair—one short and probably Mexican, the other long and smelling of buffalo grease. It could have belonged to an Apache from a band other than Lipan, but which? And it was too fresh for them to have gone far enough north for him to be Cheyenne or some other northern Plains tribe. Milton wondered about a Lipan being with Comanche. Kiowa and Comanche ran together, but not Lipan and Comanche. This would be another of the thousands of unsolved mysteries of the plains.

The tall man continued to run in his steady, dogtrot pace. The Indians had increased their speed, but he would catch them before they bedded down for the night. He bet they would be a little more careful about lighting morning fires from now on.

The Comanche hated to leave their dead behind. But this wasn't a case of running out on the dead and leaving them behind for good. After the white man had been taken care of, they would backtrack and pick up all of their dead. Or what the buzzards and other scavengers of the plains had left behind. A man should be buried by his own people so his soul would be able to rest in peace. Even the Lipan deserved this honor.

Run-to-water sat his horse a moment, watching the lone figure run toward him. Who was this man who ran like the men of old? he asked himself for the hundredth time. Even the bandy-legged Comanche of the mountains ran long distances before they came down out of the mountains to the Great Plains astride the white man's horse. But this man was not an Indian. He was dark like one, but his features were that of a white man. Not Mexican white but the white of those who came from what the Mexicans called "norteamerica." He was from that tribe of men the Indians in the north spoke of so badly. This man was tall like those Indians he had seen in the north. Tall like some Shawnee he had seen. Maybe this man was not white at all, or not all white. Maybe he was one of the native people from where the white man had come across the sea, if there was such a thing. And why should there not be? The black man had come from across the sea, so why not a red-white man?

From the great distance the chief could not tell for sure, but he could not see any scalps tied to Tall One's belt. He was sure this great warrior had made many coups and taken many lives. Run-to-water knew that most white men took scalps. Why not this one? Tall One did one strange thing that puzzled the chief. He went to each man he had killed and looked long into the dead man's face. Was he stealing the man's *puha*, his power? The most important possession of a Comanche, and something he worked for all of his life, was power. If this man was stealing it . . . A cold shiver of apprehension shook the chief.

He turned his horse and followed his men, deep in thought of what his next move should be. It had to be good, or Tall One would soon kill all of his men.

Chapter Twenty

Milton sat and waited patiently for dawn. To most men it would have seemed ages since he had left San Antonio and Velia's bed. It was not so with Milton. He accepted life as it came to him if there was no way of controlling it. Like most men who lived a rough life, whether it be on the frontiers of ancient Rome or the New World, he lived by a code and philosophy all his own. And though this was a new frontier, the men still had some links with the frontiersmen of old. Times had changed in many ways, but there was one thing they all had in common: They took life as it came, and they took from each day what enjoyment they could. At present he took enjoyment from the fact that he was sitting in the predawn cold with his rifle and not staked spread-eagle on top of some anthill.

He smiled to himself, thinking of Velia and others like her from whom he had taken much pleasure. Yes, a man took his pleasures where he found them. He was a damned fool if he passed up any on the way and let some religion or morality talk him out of enjoying them to the fullest. When things got bad for a man, he couldn't spend his time crying about his bad luck. He did the best he could with what he had, even if it hurt. Most men couldn't take the pain with the pleasure. They were not the type who would run day after day, even for the best of reasons. They wouldn't give all because of the immediate pain and discomfort, even for the long-term reward of rescuing young Josephine. The thing to remember was to gut it out, and after it was all over, he would not remember the pain. It was painful to run behind the Comanche after Josephine, but the pleasure of completing his mission was going to be Milton's reward, and the pain would be forgotten.

Huh, he grunted! He was thinking like a backwoods philosopher. He attributed this to all the reading he had done as a young boy. His red grandfather wanted him to learn as much as possible about the "other world."

The Comanche had stopped in the middle of a mound city of prairie squirrels for the night. Milton could hear the squirrels scurrying around underneath him in their tunneled city. They had given out a few barks like small dogs when he first arrived, peering out of the numerous holes around him. After their curiosity had been satisfied, they accepted his presence. He made an effort not to cover any of the little animals' exit and entrance holes.

The next morning, before dawn, a sound came from the Comanche camp that woke Milton. He cocked his rifle and waited.

The chief had ordered his men not to light fires on this morning. So each man had cooked a piece of meat the night before. The chief had warned every man to be as quiet as possible. He didn't want to lose any more men, especially since he had lost his best rifleman when the Lipan was killed. That Tall One with the sharp eye was still around with that long rifle that never missed, waiting for someone to make a mistake. Maybe the old *pubakut* was right. It could be true that an evil spirit abided in the liver of Tall One. But the chief said nothing to the men of his concern.

Maybe Tall One could see in the dark and shoot them anyway, one of the braves was heard to comment. At that moment a pheasant hidden under a tumbleweed for the night was frightened by a horse that had nearly stepped on it. It flew with a flutter of wings that roused the entire band.

Someone made the mistake the chief had feared. Milton fired at the sudden flash of the rifle. The young brave missed his target. Milton did not miss.

The friends of the wounded brave picked him up and strapped him to his horse. He would have to chew on a piece of rawhide until they came to a water hole and stopped. The Comanche rode off, bent low or lying on the backs of their mounts so the tall man could not tell which was mounted and which was not. They had learned to respect his long rifle. Only young Josephine rode upright. Milton could easily distinguish her from her outline against the light blue of the early-morning sky.

Milton fell in behind them in his even, mile-eating dogtrot. He would have liked to have gotten in one more shot, but he knew that would be pressing his luck. The Comanche had lost too many men for them to continue on docilely as if nothing was happening. He could not understand why they had not made an all-out attack on him. If they made an all-out attack they would lose two or three men. If he were lucky, they would lose five. After his single-shot rifle had been fired, and the one round from his pistol, it would be a hand-to-hand fight if he could get in close. But they didn't even have to risk a hand-to-hand confrontation. They could ride around him at a distance and fill him full of arrows like a woman's pin cushion. At this rate he could pick them off one at a time. He knew they feared his rifle, but not enough to hold them at bay this long. Something was holding them back, and it was not fear of death and battle. These were Comanche.

The Comanche rode along wondering what to do about Tall One. The warriors no longer felt they had enough power to match this enemy. Without power, there was no use in trying to force an issue. A man must have power, personal power, if he were to stand against a spirit.

The old medicine man looked over his shoulder so often that the chief also began to look back. All of the young braves had listened to the old *puhakut*'s talk, and they knew that he was right. Who but an evil spirit could have guided Tall One's rifle ball straight and true in the dark when one could hardly see? This had been done twice. Only once could it be considered an accident. Who but a man with a spirit to shield him could have so many arrows and bullets miss him? Who but a man with a spirit, good or bad, could run day after day across the plains?

Maybe they could not kill this man. As the young warriors became more and more nervous the chief became more and more worried. He knew that no one could handle a bunch of excited Comanche warriors.

By midmorning the band had reached another water hole. It was like coming upon an oasis in the desert, with scrub brush and mesquite trees taking the place of date palms. There was even a stunted willow and a stand of prickly pear cactus as large as a small house. It was obvious that this was a large, permanent water hole with a year-round source. Other water holes that Milton had found on the Llano had little or no vegetation. Unless the holes were known, it was nearly impossible to find them in this flat country. Most of them were thick from sand and mud, stirred up by buffalo using them as wallows.

A doe and her two fawns, using the prickly pear for shade, bounded off in fright as the men approached. The sudden movement by the deer caused horses to buck and men to shout in excitement. But no young braves rode out after the deer in a whooping, hell-bent-for-the-kill chase. They were a much subdued group for a band of Comanche of the Kwaharie clan. The young braves had convinced themselves, with plenty of talk and rumor, that a man with an evil spirit followed them.

The braves stood to one side in a group talking among themselves, leaving one man to attend the wounded. The old *puhakut* walked to the group of men and listened to their complaints. Finally the younger braves were joined by the older men. It was the custom of the Comanche that in council all warriors, regardless of their age, had a right to speak. But often a short powwow was held so men could air their complaints to one who would be their spokesman. Rolling Bush was selected as the spokesman for these braves. Not only was he respected by all, he was among the few who would brave a face-to-face confrontation with Run-to-water. After the short powwow Rolling Bush joined Run-to-water, who stood alone looking impassively across the hot prairie.

"I must speak to you on an important matter that concerns all of us," Rolling Bush announced in a formal manner.

"Speak," Run-to-water commanded with more of a grunt than with words.

"We have lost many men on this raid. Everything was good until the tall one began to follow us. We have stolen many fine horses and mules from the white ones. A young girl who is strong of spirit and strong of limb for some young brave, or to be traded, has been captured. Now things have gone bad, Run-to-water. It is not your fault. One of an evil spirit follows us. My medicine bag to make great medicine is at the main camp in my tepee. I am powerless to protect us from his evil spirit. Give him the girl, Run-to-water. Give him the horses if he asks. Our lives are in your hands, Run-to-water. Only a wise chief can save us."

Run-to-water continued to stare out over the prairie. He stood immobile and stone-faced. It seemed as if he had not heard a word Rolling Bush had said. Then he said, "No, I will not give up the captive."

Rolling Bush was not finished. "Give her up, Run-to-water. Give up this white girl. The people will not blame you. They will have Tall One and his evil spirit to blame. All know there is no protection from one with a strong evil spirit. You will not be blamed, Run-to-water. Hear me. You will not be blamed."

The old *puhakut* was only partly right. Some of the braves would convince themselves that Tall One did, indeed, possess an evil spirit. They would blame all their misfortunes and bad luck on this man. But others would not believe, or not want to believe, and they would question his ability as a leader. Even if they believed some of the talk, they would blame him, Run-to-water, for their failures. It was a simple problem of maneuvering for leadership and clan politics.

Even those who wished to displace him would have to consider Comanche customs and heritage. It was believed by their people that when an evil spirit entered the bodies of some men, they were indeed too powerful to be controlled by a mere man, even if this man was a great war chief. This belief could not be pushed aside. But his enemies would still use this trouble with Tall One in the future. A man stayed in the position of chief to the Comanche as long as he himself was a powerful warrior in the field and a good field general. He had to have the respect of every man in his war party or raiding party. Even if they didn't like him, the leader must have their respect.

Run-to-water was also concerned about what the members and leaders of the other clans would think. A man cannot sit in council when he has lost face. It is too humiliating. On the other hand, if Rolling Bush was able to convince everyone that there was, in truth, an evil spirit in Tall One's liver, and the story was acceptable to all, then that would be a different matter. But there were still those who would think that Tall One was simply a good warrior. And to be subdued by one man was unthinkable.

He had a problem.

This old man beside him was not only his mother's brother but had been a friend since he was a young boy. Rolling Bush was one of the most respected men in the tribe. If anyone could make the men believe it was true about the evil spirit, it was Rolling Bush. Still, it was hard to surrender.

"No! I will not give up the captive!" Run-to-water said, determined not to give up without a fight.

"Think, man, think! With a man who has an evil spirit, you will not be blamed for what has happened. No one can fight an evil spirit without proper things. I have asked for a *tavevekut*, "a sun-killing," but the sun has not heard me and will not pass and execute judgment. You must give the girl to him. Give her up, Run-to-water, and let him take her back to her people. We cannot let him follow us to our camp."

"No! I will talk of it no more!" There was finality in the chief's voice.

Although Run-to-water called the old man *Ara*, "uncle," a man's mother's brother, all knew that when the chief had said he would "talk no more," no one had better speak. Run-to-

water had been known to kill when angered, and he did not
stop to figure out the relationship.

The old *puhakut* shrugged his shoulders and returned to tell
the other braves that they would move on. The girl and horses
would remain with them. Some of the men were pleased, some
were not.

A young warrior shouted, "Then I will go, alone! I will
leave this group. I will find another to follow!" He jumped on
the back of his horse.

"Waspfighter! You are speaking to your leader!" he was reminded.

Waspfighter, contempt written across his face, kicked his
horse forward. He brought the animal to a sliding halt in front
of Run-to-water. "I will find a leader who thinks more of the
lives of his men than of his own vanity!"

Run-to-water grabbed the leather thong reins of the horse
and jerked down and to his left. With a scream of fright, the
horse was flipped over on its side. Waspfighter jumped free
and scrambled out of the way on all fours. Run-to-water strode
after him and kicked him in the side, forcing the wind out of
the warrior. Then the chief kicked him in the head. The dazed
warrior lay in the hot sand, gasping for breath.

Run-to-water turned to the rest of the men. "I am the leader.
I decide what we will and will not do!" he said. "No one
commands me, Run-to-water, to do anything! If that man tries,
he must win it by honor."

The chief looked around at the men, taking the measure of
each. "Any man who wishes to gain his leadership by honor
must meet me on the field of battle to the death. I will meet
any takers. But my position will not be challenged—by anyone!"

Without another word Run-to-water jumped on the back of
his horse. "Now we ride!" he growled.

Chapter Twenty-one

Run-to-water didn't look back to see whether the men followed. He would take care of any more insubordination in the manner of a Comanche leader, with a firmness that allowed no give and take.

The men mounted their horses and rode with angry, sullen looks on their faces. They were close to rebellion and ready to take the girl back to Tall One themselves. Defiance of a chief was nothing new or strange to a Comanche.

Rolling Bush surveyed all of this with a wary eye. He had seen men in numbers fall upon a powerful chief they did not like and kill him. If the number of those conspiring together was large enough, who was to say they were wrong? Power was the all-powerful element to the Comanche. Something had to be done to cool these hotheads. He had his job cut out for him.

As they continued to ride, the men rode in small groups. Every once in a while the spokesman for his particular group would ride to another group to compare notes.

Run-to-water didn't have to worry that his young braves would try to set up ambushes for Tall One. They feared and hated this man, and they would keep a healthy distance from him. All the chief had to worry about now was keeping his young braves from running wild back to the main camp.

As they rode, they continued to look over their shoulders at the man following them. Tall One moved along the ground as though he didn't need legs. The small cloud of dust stirred up by his feet seemed to propel him along, and he didn't need to run to keep up with them.

Run-to-water forced himself to look straight ahead. He wanted to turn and look, but to do so would be a sign of weakness. And he was not a weak man. But he not only wanted to turn and look, he wanted to turn and charge the white man, screaming out his frustration and defiance in his final charge—and he knew that it would be his final charge. He knew that he had more than he could handle following him. An evil spirit. A spirit that would affect his entire clan, his entire nation, if he was allowed to continue to follow them. All would be lost. The seed of his people would be no more!

The chief shook his head violently to clear it. He was getting as bad as everyone else.

Rolling Bush had been watching the chief closely. He could see that the man following them was beginning to have an effect on Run-to-water. The minds of mere men can do strange things to them at times, even the strong ones. He knew. He also knew that it was time for him to make his move.

The old *puhakut* rode up alongside Run-to-water. "We are in a dilemma, Nephew. A very bad one."

"That is true," Run-to-water conceded.

"Can I give you advice?" Rolling Bush asked. "Not as your uncle but as your *puhakut?*"

"You know I always have time for advice from a *puhakut.* I always seek the counsel of such men. Even more so, you, my uncle, who is the greatest of all *puhakuts*," Run-to-water told him. The old man may give him a good way out of this confusing problem.

"You know that we cannot allow a man with an evil spirit to be killed or to die in this land of ours," the old man told him. "If by some means we kill him or he is accidentally wiped out by a freak of nature, we don't know where his evil spirit may go when it leaves his body. It is a problem that has taken much thought."

"Yes, it is a problem," Run-to-water agreed.

"If we let him follow to our main camp, where I do have the means to conquer this spirit of his, I may not be quick enough," Rolling Bush told him. He took another quick look

over his shoulder. "If that happens, who knows what damage
he may do to our people before he is controlled! It is a great
problem."

Run-to-water only grunted.

"I will speak of this to the other *puhakut*s, of the problem
you had on this trip. I will speak of this in council," the old
man told his nephew. He would do his best to protect and give
aid to his favorite nephew.

Run-to-water suddenly pulled back on the reins of his horse.
He had made a decision.

"You are right, old one. We must not think of ourselves, as
warriors have a tendency to do. We must also think of all of
our people. That is the role of a leader," Run-to-water told
him. "And, Uncle, I am not a vain man."

The chief turned his horse and rode back to the men.

The old *puhakut* smiled.

When the Indians halted, Milton stopped also. He leaned on
his rifle and took a drink of water. His eyes swept the area in
search of the best spot for a defense. There was none. It all
looked the same, level and grassy.

The chief didn't say a word to anyone. He rode over to the
subchief and took the lead rope of the girl's mule. Leading the
mule, he rode toward Milton, his hand raised in the universal
sign of peace.

Milton stood leaning on his rifle. From all outward appear-
ances he looked as if he were in no danger and had nothing to
fear. But inside, his nerves and reflexes were coiled as tight as
the main spring of a Swiss-made clock. He had no fear of the
chief, for he knew that, above all, a Comanche was like most
red men. He would not betray a man once his word was given,
and he was traveling under the sign of peace. But Milton did
worry about the young braves. They had not given their word
on anything. He knew well the temperament of the Comanche
and that they could not always be controlled by their leaders.
They were an independent bunch who didn't mind fighting
among themselves if no one else was handy. They were as bad
about that as the white man. The Comanche did have one

virtue the white men failed to exercise however: They did not steal from each other.

The chief rode up to Milton and stopped his horse. Milton took a quick look at the girl to make sure she was all right before turning his attention to the Indian chief. The girl was past the point of caring and sat her mule tiredly. The past few days of fourteen and fifteen hours of continuous riding without pause had taken its toll on her physically. Her only break on the march had been when she was allowed to pause long enough to relieve herself when nature called. And often the tight rawhide thongs were not untied even then.

"Senor, I come in peace," Run-to-water called out in Spanish.

"Speak. I will listen," Milton replied in Comanche.

The chief looked at Milton with new interest. Not many white men bothered to learn the language of the Comanche. It had always been that if an Indian wished to talk to a white man, he had to learn Spanish. But this man was not Mexican. He must be like old Missing-two-toes had said. This man was one of those Yanquis from the east country. The chief looked closer. Yes, this man was a Yanqui. His looks were not Mexican, and his eyes were blue like the winter sky.

"I am called Run-to-water by my people," the chief told him.

"I am called Tladatsidihi, 'Panther Killer,' by my people," Milton said, giving his Indian name.

When Milton was a boy of eleven years of age he and two other boys were playing near a small stream. A panther on the other side of the creek jumped from its tree and stood on the opposite bank watching them. Milton had grabbed his small spear and stood, fearlessly waiting for the big cat to act. The panther charged, springing in the air to clear the water. Milton stuck the butt of the spear into the ground and the panther landed on its point. It went through the animal's body before the shaft broke. Milton joined the other boys up in a tree to watch the panther jump and bite at the spear sticking through its body until it died. It was then that he was given that name, which had held. He also carried one of its teeth in his medicine bag. The name he was given at birth would remain a secret, never to be revealed for fear an enemy might use it to defeat him by some witchery. There were many things in his Indian training that his white man's training could not replace.

"To us you are known as Tall One."

Milton shook his head that he understood and accepted this name.

"I come, Tall One, to give you the girl," Run-to-water said bluntly.

"Why do you do this? I am only one and you are many," Milton said. He again checked the men behind the chief. All were waiting.

The chief looked closely at Milton. No, this man was not white, or at least not all white. He was a breed. Not like the Mexican, as he had first known. Most of the Mexican breeds were squat and dark. This man was tall and straight. He was tall like the Shawnee he had once seen.

"We do not want this girl. Look at her! Seven days on the trail and look at her. She looks like an old woman, not a young woman who has just come into her time. All her children would be runts and weak like her. The milk from her breasts would not be strong to keep them alive, or to make strong warriors. We would have to milk a mare to feed her young ones, or get a camp bitch dog. None of my young men want her for a wife. The Mescalero would not give us much for this girl. The Lipan would give even less. The Kiowa would not want her at all. She cannot even cook.

"Here, take her, Tall One," Run-to-water urged, offering him the lead rope of the mule. "Take her to her mother so she can be cared for. We will give her to you, and her mule, so you may get her home alive."

Milton walked over to the girl, looking her and the mule up and down as if he were bargaining for her. For the first time she looked up. A ray of hope flashed across her face before she dropped her eyes again. Milton looked at the chief, his face emotionless and noncommittal. "You give me a tired girl on an equally tired mule. Do you wish to keep us slow so we cannot travel as quickly as the Comanche? So we may not follow you? You must have very little thought of yourselves as warriors."

He looked at the chief, whose face remained impassive. The Comanche war chief was an expert at psychological facial confrontations, and Milton would not know what effect the words had upon the Indian. The chief had given his reason for giving up the girl—he thought her worthless. Now Milton had interjected a new reason. She was being given to him because the Comanche feared him as a warrior. He may have hit a raw nerve, but he could not tell by looking into the eyes of the chief. Milton knew that one never looked an Indian in the eye to read the effect of his words. An Indian's face would remain as expressionless as the face of a rock even as he informed you that he was going to gut you and feed your testicles to the village dogs.

"Then we will give her a better mount," Run-to-water said, ignoring Milton's comment.

Run-to-water used sign language to command that a horse be brought forward. A young brave brought one.

Milton eyed the horse, then walked over to the girl and lifted her off the jaded mule. He took her saddle off the mule and put it on the fresh horse. She had been kept on a tired mule so that she could not manage to escape, though it is doubtful she could ever have gotten very far. Her wrists had been kept tied mainly out of cruelty.

After he had cut the rawhide thongs that bound her wrists, Milton picked up the girl and sat her on the fresh animal. He looked at the chief. Now he would know whether he had a hold or some type of power over the Comanche. "Do you expect a warrior to walk like a squaw while a woman rides?"

The chief hesitated a moment, then signaled for another horse.

There was grumbling behind them, but a young brave brought another horse forward. He dropped the lead rope on the ground. He would not hand the rope to an enemy who was responsible for killing six of his friends. That same man had now added insult to injury by not only taking the girl but two of their horses as well. The young warrior looked at Tall One with open hatred. He was young and had not yet learned to keep his feelings hidden. With a jerk on his reins, he wheeled his horse and rode back to join his friends, giving out blood-curdling whoops of defiance.

Milton easily jumped astride the saddleless horse. He did not appear any worse for wear after his ordeal of tracking the raiding party on foot. If necessary, he could run five or six days more without a long break. But what did not show externally was felt internally. The balls of his feet were sore, the inside of his thighs had rubbed raw, and the muscles in the back of his thighs were still aching. It had taken most of the morning for his stomach to settle down after that first day of running. He was not in the same physical shape as when he was a young man. He had become too dependent on the horse, and his lower extremities were weak from lack of use. He would have to start running more to keep himself in shape.

The girl was now at his side, and if they could get out of the Llano Estacado alive, she would be home with her family in a few days. He knew that he could get out alive, and he had faith in her. She had gone through a lot and still held up.

Now he would ask for one more thing, and it would be his last. A man could push another one just so far, and then even death would begin to seem like a better price to pay than more loss of face.

"How do you expect a warrior to cross a waterless land without water for a weak woman?" he asked, making it a point to bring up the need for water on the woman's behalf and not for himself.

For the first time Run-to-water showed some sign of his feelings in his eyes. The expression was a flash across his eyes that faded immediately. His face remained as immobile as stone. He raised his hand and signaled for water. There was a cry of anger and defiance. The negative response was unanimous. Without looking back he again signaled for water, and again received the same response.

Rolling Bush rode out from the group and came forward. He rode proudly, straight of back, sitting his horse as easily as a young man. It was hard to tell from his appearance that the old man was now in his sixty-eighth summer on the Llano Estacado. Everyone who knew the old warrior, be they friend or foe, respected him. There were too few men of his type in the world to Milton's way of thinking, and he could not help admiring the old gentleman.

The old *puhakut* rode up beside Milton and sat his horse for a moment. There was no anger or hatred in his eyes, for he had also begun to admire Milton as a warrior and a man. He thought Milton was one of the very few of his kind. And because he respected the outstanding qualities of a warrior in a man and his ability for survival, Rolling Bush did not want to see this man's blood or seed wasted upon the hot sands of the prairie. He handed his water bag to the tall man. "May you take the evil spirit with you from this land, Tall One."

Now Milton knew why he was being given the girl and a way out. The old *puhakut* had convinced the rest of the men that he had an evil spirit. That was the old man's way of explaining to them their failure to kill him. It was also the old man's way of explaining why he could not protect them. No one questioned the power of a spirit. Milton knew now that he would be able to get out of the Llano Estacado alive. If he died on the plains, his evil spirit would remain to haunt the Comanche. A dead spirit was one kind of trouble the Comanche didn't need. The other thing that would be his ticket out was the water bag he held. It had the sign of the *puhakut* on it, and no one would touch him. No Comanche, that is. Now if they just didn't run into any Kiowa. . . .

"You are not a white man. Who are you? Are you a native people from the other side of the great salt water?" Rolling Bush asked. He was always the inquisitive one, which seemed to be the mentality of medicine men the world over. Rolling Bush was willing to talk of ethnic backgrounds.

"I am a breed, white, and of the Ani-Yuwiya, the 'Principal People,' " Milton told him. "We are of the Ugayu, the 'Seven-clan society.' "

"That cannot be so. We are Nemenuh, The People. You cannot be The People," Rolling Bush objected. "We are The People!"

Every ancient people call themselves "The People," "The Human Beings," or similar terms to signify that they were the select creation of God. That is one of the reasons members of one tribe would not call another tribe by its own tribal designation. That was certainly the reason white Christians refused to use tribal designations.

"We are not The People. We are the Principal People," Milton told the *puhakut*. When it came to tribal pride, Milton was as vain as any full-blooded Cherokee who ever lived. He would claim his white blood when it was most convenient, not because he was ashamed of his Cherokee heritage. The Cherokee called other Indians Ani-Yuwuya, "People," and he called the white man simply Unaka, "White." The Cherokee never said that other men were not human beings, simply that others were only "People" and the Cherokee were of a higher order.

"I have never heard of these Yuwiya," Rolling Bush said, a smirk on his face. No one was going to tell him to his face that they were Principal People while he was something less.

" 'Ani-Yuwiya' is the plural form," Milton informed him.

"Well, I've never heard of any of those people," the old man said with disgust.

"We are called Chiluk-ki, 'People of the Cave Country,' by the Choctaw. The white people call us Cherokee, which is their way of saying 'Chiluk-ki'." Milton told him, giving him a lesson in Eastern American Indian culture.

Rolling Stone wasn't buying this Principal People business. He would go along with "Cherokee" or some other word.

"Some say that the white man is not able to say many Indian words and that they are not very smart," Rolling Bush said with a smug look on his face.

"Some say this is true." Milton was glad to agree with him.

"Do all of these men called Cherokee have blue eyes?" asked Rolling Bush.

"I have a grandfather who is a white man," Milton admitted.

"That is a pity. You could have been a great warrior if you had been all Indian," Rolling Bush said, clucking his tongue.

"White blood hasn't tainted me too much," Milton said bluntly.

"We are called Comanche by the Mexicans," Rolling Bush informed Milton. "It is from the Ute word *Komantcia*, 'someone who wants to fight me all the time.' We are great warriors, Tall One."

Milton nodded that he would agree with that statement.

Run-to-water had never seen such a display of egotism as he had seen from these two. But he had to admit, he had not seen many who had as much right.

Rolling Bush pulled his horse around and rode to Run-to-water's side. He had said all he wished to say, and now he sat his horse passively.

"I will give no more," Run-to-water told Milton. Every man has to be left a way out. "I refuse to give anything else. The conversation is ended."

Milton nodded his head that he understood.

Run-to-water turned his horse and rode off.

Rolling Bush looked at Milton. "Tall One, do not ride into our country again and expect your evil spirit to protect you. I have strong medicine in my tepee. It will take away your protection. Then you will be a common warrior again like the rest of us. This is Comanche land, Tall One. Tell the white men that it will remain Comanche land forever."

The old man started to turn his horse. He stopped and looked at Milton. A sudden sadness filled his eyes. "Tall One, do not come back to Comanche land. I had a dream last night. I saw Tall One with many white men. I saw Tall One killed. He was killed by Comanche. A young warrior rode into camp with Tall One's scalp tied to his war lance and he cried out, 'I

have killed Tall One! Now I will find a white woman and she
will carry my seed in her belly to make a great Comanche war
chief.' You will have to pay for this gift of the girl, Tall One.
Do not come back to Comanche land."

Rolling Bush turned and rode his horse back to his men.

For the first time in his life, a cold hand gripped the heart of
Milton Hicks. He had been educated by the white man and
instructed in Christianity—which didn't take hold—by missionaries. But there was enough Cherokee blood in him to
respect the *puhakut*s of the world. He had seen too many "medicine men" of his own people who could predict the future
accurately. Most of those predictions came through dreams,
which he was a great believer in himself. Milton would remember this warning, but it would not change his manner of
acting. If called to enter the land of the Comanche again, he
would not hesitate to do so.

The two Comanche leaders rode to their men, never looking
back. The men fell in behind them with the rest of the captured horses and mules.

Three young braves broke away from the group and rode
their horses straight toward Milton and Josephine. Milton sat
still and did not take his rifle from the crook of his arm.

"Steady, girl, steady," he told Josephine.

There was a look of terror on her face, but Milton's calm
voice reassured her.

The three braves broke to the left when they got close and
circled the two, brandishing war lances and making short, yip-
ping war cries. One of the braves was the one who had given
Milton an open look of hatred when he had brought the horse
to him. If the young warrior lived to be an adult, Milton was
sure that he would be one of the best warriors in the tribe.

After they had made one complete circle, they rode back to
the group with their usual display of superb horsemanship.
One young brave passed completely under his pony's belly
from right to left. He was under his mount when it jumped a
growth of tumbleweed. The horse never broke stride, and the
young brave completed his maneuver.

Milton watched them ride away. The Comanche was indeed, as Jean du Bois called them, the Tatars of the Plains. He went where and when he wished, the buffalo providing him with all his needs. He fended off encroachment upon his domain by the white man with a savage fury that frightened, repulsed, and brought respect from his enemy. These plains were his homeland and his alone, and like the Tatar, he used the horse at his command to keep it that way. He would share this land with no one except his cousin, the Kiowa.

They were a proud people, these Comanche, and like all men who have little else, they placed high value on that pride. Some of the physical symbols of their pride that could be seen and felt were the plains and the buffalo. They were willing to die for them. But the days of the Comanche were numbered, Milton knew. The land-hungry Americans were coming. They were already in Texas. If they couldn't cheat or steal the land from the red man, they would kill him off or remove him. These people would lose, like all others.

Ride on, warriors of the plains, for your time is near its end, thought Milton, a sadness in his heart. He turned his pony and rode to the southwest. The girl followed without a word.